学术顾问

（以姓氏笔画为序）

王　宏　冯智文　李正栓　李丽生　原一川

Academic Advisors

Wang Hong　Feng Zhiwen　Li Zhengshuan

Li Lisheng　Yuan Yichuan

主　编

李昌银

副主编

黄　瑛　彭庆华

General Editor

Li Changyin

Professor of English　Yunnan Normal University

Associate General Editors

Huang Ying

Professor of English　Yunnan Normal University

Peng Qinghua

Professor of English　Yunnan Normal University

云南少数民族经典作品英译文库
Classics of Yunnan Ethnic Groups in English Translation

主编 李昌银 General Editor Li Changyin
副主编 黄瑛 彭庆华 Associate General Editors Huang Ying & Peng Qinghua

Ebing and Sangluo

娥并与桑洛

整理◎云南省民族民间文学德宏调查队
英译◎刘德周
译校◎［美］包琼

Edited by the Dehong Collecting Team of Yunnan Ethnic Folklore
Translated by Liu Dezhou
Revised by Joan Cecile Boulerice

云南出版集团
云南人民出版社

图书在版编目（CIP）数据

娥并与桑洛 ：汉、英 / 云南省民族民间文学德宏调查队整理 ；刘德周英译. -- 昆明 ：云南人民出版社，2020.2

（云南少数民族经典作品英译文库 / 李昌银主编）

ISBN 978-7-222-19074-0

Ⅰ. ①娥… Ⅱ. ①云… ②刘… Ⅲ. ①傣族—叙事诗—中国—汉、英 Ⅳ. ①I222.7

中国版本图书馆CIP数据核字(2020)第028257号

出 品 人 李 维 赵石定
项目统筹 周 祥 殷筱钊
项目组稿 郭木玉
责任编辑 郭木玉 明 珍
装帧设计 马 滨 石 斌
责任校对 王琳淇 溥 思 费 珺
责任印制 陆卫华 代隆参

云南少数民族经典作品英译文库
Classics of Yunnan Ethnic Groups in English Translation

娥并与桑洛
Ebing and Sangluo

整理◎云南省民族民间文学德宏调查队
英译◎刘德周
译校◎［美］包琼

Edited by the Dehong Collecting Team of Yunnan Ethnic Folklore
Translated by Liu Dezhou
Revised by Joan Cecile Boulerice

出 版 云南出版集团 云南人民出版社
发 行 云南人民出版社
社 址 昆明市环城西路609号
邮 编 650034
网 址 www.ynpph.com.cn
E-mail ynrms@sina.com
开 本 787mm×1092mm 1/16
印 张 14
字 数 190千
版 次 2020年2月第1版第1次印刷
印 刷 云南出版印刷集团有限责任公司 云南新华印刷一厂
书 号 ISBN 978-7-222-19074-0
定 价 75.00元

云南人民出版社
微信公众号

序 一

◎李正栓

民族典籍英译是传播中国文化、文学和文明的重要途径，是中华文化走出去的重要组成部分。文化与文学的传播，是一个国家提高文化软实力的重要方式，在文化交流和文明建设中起着不可或缺的作用，对提高国家对外话语权、构建国家对外话语体系以及对建设世界文学都有积极意义。

中国各少数民族拥有许多优秀的典籍，具有很高的文物价值、文学价值和文化价值。各民族的先人们通过口头流传或用文字记述了他们各具特色的文化。各少数民族几乎都有自己民族的创世史、史诗和神话传说。

中国民族典籍独具特色，不可替代。重视民族典籍的翻译和研究工作，对于挖掘各民族优秀文化，保护各民族文明，增强各民族之间的沟通和了解，进一步向世界其他地区传播各少数民族优秀文化，乃至提高我国文化软实力都有着重要意义。不少少数民族聚居地处于祖国边疆，有的处在“一带一路”建设关键部位，有的处在与周边国家进行各种交流的重要位置。

中国民族典籍是世界多元文化的有机组成部分，与其他文化共同造就了世界文化的绚丽多姿。世界正因为其文化多样性才变得缤纷多彩。我国各民族典籍中包含的文化多样性极大地丰富了世界多元、特色鲜明的文化。人们对多样性形成全新的认识角度和思维方式。多样性开阔了人们的视野，丰富了人们思考问题的角度。挖掘这些典籍中所蕴含的教育价值和文化价值，对世界其他民族都有指导和借鉴意义，并且有助于建设我国的文化自信。

民族典籍本身蕴含的特殊价值对加强民族文化了解、促进中外文化交流具有重大意义。民族典籍英译具有文学翻译和文化传递之功能，有对外宣传作用，还是一种文学外交。因此，民族典籍翻译和研究对于维护祖国统一、促进民族团结、稳定边疆以及增强国内各民族和中外文化之间的交流都起着极为重要的作用。

中华人民共和国成立以后，中央政府一直十分重视民族典籍翻译和研究工作，提供了强有力的政策支持，并采取了一系列有效措施，加快了各少数民族典籍的抢救、整理、翻译和研究的进程。中央政府多次召开西藏工作会议和新疆工作会议。近年来，国际和国内对于多元文化高度关注，少数民族文学典籍的翻译已然成为业内研究的热点。

近年来，民族典籍翻译和研究迅猛发展，势头良好。国家大力支持，发放国家社科基金课题，教育部和国家民委也发放课题，扶持了一大批研究者。很多民族典籍翻译课题得以立项并顺利开展；为数不少的民族典籍被翻译成汉语、英语和其他语言并出版发行；越来越多的业界人士致力于这个满富生机的学术领域。

在中国文化走出去的国家战略下，全国少数民族典籍英译学术研讨会陆续召开，已经召开三次。

云南是中国民族最多的省份。人口在5000人以上的少数民族有25个，其中有15个民族为云南所特有，分别是：白族、哈尼族、傣族、傈僳族、佤族、拉祜族、纳西族、景颇族、布朗族、普米族、阿昌族、基诺族、怒族、德昂族、独龙族。其中除白族人口占全国白族人口总数的84%以上外，其他14个民族95%居住在云南。

云南还是我国跨境民族最多的省份。在云南的25个少数民族中，有16个民族跨境而居，分别是：傣族、壮族、苗族、景颇族、瑶族、哈尼族、德昂族、佤族、拉祜族、彝族、阿昌族、傈僳族、布依族、怒族、布朗族、独龙族。

云南少数民族创造了辉煌的文化。据不完全统计，云南少数民族文字文献古籍蕴藏量达10万余册（卷），口传古籍4万余种。云南省民委少数民族古籍整理出版规划办公室为了挽救和保护这些古籍，计划在5年内编纂出版100卷《云南少数民族古籍珍本集成》。这是一个令人瞩目的庞大计划。将这些古籍中的珍品翻译介绍给世界，不仅能够弘扬云南省丰富多彩的民族文化，而且有助于增进与南亚东南亚国家的理解与交流，为“一带一路”倡议的实施做出贡献。

云南师范大学外国语学院很重视这一领域的工作。在外国语学院领导支持下，李昌银教授带领一个由教授和中青年学者组成的团队对精选出来的17部云南少数民族经典作品进行英译，计划在5年内（“十三五”期间）翻译出版。这是一项十分有意义的宏大工程。

这17部民族典籍，内容全部为各民族的英雄史诗或神话传说，具有很高的历史意义和文学价值。这些作品涉及阿昌族、白族、傣族、德昂族、哈尼族、景颇族、拉祜族、苗族、纳西族、普米族、彝族等 11 个少数民族。

云南师范大学这支翻译队伍实力强大，主要由一些多年从事翻译教学、研究和实践的教授和副教授组成，他们是李昌银、黄瑛、彭庆华、孙兴文、吴相如、刘德周、杨慧芳、郜菊、陈萍、包琼（Joan Cecile Boulerice）等国内外专家学者。他们在云南翻译界都是风云人物。

在民族典籍英译中，这支队伍异军突起，为我国民族典籍英译壮大了声势，必将为中国民族典籍走向世界而成为世界文学的一部分做出新贡献。

民族典籍翻译与研究事业关乎国家的稳定统一，关乎民族关系的和谐发展，关乎世界多元文化的实现。在中国，民族典籍资源极为丰富，有待进一步挖掘、翻译。因此，民族典籍英译前景光明。同时，我们也应意识到，仍有许多濒临消失的少数民族典籍亟待拯救，民族典籍翻译与研究工作任重而道远。

（李正栓，中国英汉语比较研究会典籍英译专业委员会常务副会长兼秘书长、河北师范大学博士生导师）

Foreword by Li Zhengshuan

The translation of Chinese ethnic classics is an important approach in spreading Chinese culture, literature and civilization. It is a crucial component of Chinese culture going global. The spreading of Chinese culture and literature is a national policy and an important way to improve the cultural soft power of China. It plays an indispensable role in the cultural exchange between China and other countries and the development of world literature.

The ethnic groups in China have countless excellent classics with high anthropological, literary and cultural value. The ancestors of each ethnic group have passed down their distinctive culture orally or in writing. Almost all the ethnic groups have their own story of creation, epics, myths and legends.

Chinese ethnic classics are unique and irreplaceable. It is imperative to attach importance to the translation and research of ethnic classics; to explore the excellent ethnic cultures; to protect the civilization of ethnic groups; to enhance the communication and understanding among ethnic groups; to further spread the outstanding culture of ethnic groups to other parts of the world; and to build the cultural strength of China. Many ethnic groups live in the border areas and thus play an important role in the cultural and economic cooperation between China and its neighbors in the context of the Belt and Road Initiative.

Chinese ethnic classics are an important component of the magnificence and diversity of world culture. It is diversity that makes the world so colorful. The cultural diversity of Chinese ethnic classics has greatly enriched the world's pluralism and its distinctive features. People around the world have formed a new understanding of diversity. This diversity has expanded people's horizon and enriched their way of thinking. Digging out the educational and cultural value in these classics can contribute to the construction of China's self-confidence in culture.

The special value of the ethnic classics itself is of great significance to the strengthening of national culture and intercultural communication between China and foreign countries. The translation of ethnic classics is not just a literary exchange, but also a form of cultural communication. It is diplomacy through literature in that it consolidates the cultural ties between China and other countries.

After the founding of the People's Republic of China, the central government attached great importance to the translation and research of ethnic classics, provided a great deal of policy support, and adopted a series of effective measures to speed up the process of rescuing, collating, translating and studying ethnic classics. The central government has convened several working conferences on Tibet and Xinjiang. In recent years, both China and other countries have paid close attention to multiculture. The translation of ethnic classics has become a hot topic.

In recent years, the translation and research of ethnic classics have progressed rapidly and have shown good prospects. The government strongly supports and grants the research projects of the national social science fund. The Ministry of Education and the State Ethnic Affairs Commission are also issuing research projects and giving funding to a large number of researchers. Many research projects on ethnic classics have been approved and carried out. Many ethnic classics have been translated into Chinese, English and other languages and published. More and more professionals have dedicated themselves to this new sphere of learning.

In this context, the academic conferences on translation of ethnic classics are held one after another all around the country. And up to now three have been held.

Yunnan is the province which has the most ethnic groups in China. Besides the Han people, there are 25 ethnic groups, each with a population of more than 5,000. Among them, 15 ethnic groups are unique to Yunnan, which are the Bai, the Hani, the Dai, the Lisu, the Wa, the Lahu, the Naxi, the Jingpo, the Bulang, the Pumi, the Achang, the Jinuo, the Nu, the De'ang and the Dulong. Among these, 84% of the total number of the Bai people in China and 95% of the other 14 ethnic groups are living in Yunnan.

Yunnan is also the province which has the most cross-border ethnic groups. Of the 25 ethnic groups, 16 live across the border, namely: the Dai, the Zhuang, the Miao, the Jingpo, the Yao, the Hani, the De'ang, the Wa, the Lahu, the Yi, the Achang, the Lisu, the Buyi, the Nu, the Bulang and the Dulong.

The ethnic groups in Yunnan have created splendid cultures. According to statistics, the number of classics of Yunnan ethnic groups is more than 100 thousand volumes and classics in oral tradition are more than 40 thousand. In order to save and protect these ancient books, the Office of Classics Collation and Publishing of Yunnan Ethnic Groups Affairs Commission planned to compile and publish 100 volumes of *A Collection of Yunnan Ethnic Group Rare Books* in five years, which is an ambitious plan. The introduction of the ancient classics via translation can not only promote and develop the colorful ethnic cultures of Yunnan, but also contribute to the understanding and exchange between China and countries in South Asia and Southeast Asia and to the implementation of the Belt and Road Initiative as well.

The School of Foreign Languages and Literature of Yunnan Normal University is paying close attention to this field. With the support of the School and the University,

Professor Li Changyin is leading a group of professors and young scholars to do the project of *Classics of Yunnan Ethnic Groups in English Translation*, which includes 17 ethnic classics selected carefully from Yunnan's bountiful ethnic classics. These books are the heroic epics or myths and legends of each ethnic groups with great historical significance and literary value. They will finish the translation in five years (during the Thirteenth Five-Year Plan). After that, all the works will be published by Yunnan People's Publishing House.

The 17 works cover 11 ethnic groups: the Achang, the Bai, the Dai, the De'ang, the Hani, the Jingpo, the Lahu, the Miao, the Naxi, the Pumi and the Yi. All of these groups except the Miao and the Yi are unique to Yunnan.

The translation team of Yunnan Normal University is full of strength and vitality, composed of professors and associate professors who have been occupied in translation teaching, research, and practice for a long time. They are Li Changyin, Huang Ying, Peng Qinghua, Sun Xingwen, Wu Xiangru, Liu Dezhou, Yang Huifang, Gao Ju, Chen Ping, Joan Boulerice and other experts and scholars who are representative figures in the translation field in Yunnan province.

This team is a new force that has suddenly arisen in terms of translating ethnic classics. It is expanding the momentum of ethnic classics translation in China and has made a new contribution for China's ethnic classics to go global and become a part of world literature.

The translation and research of ethnic classics are related to the development of Chinese culture and the realization of multiculturalism in the world. In China, ethnic classics are extremely rich in resources, which require us to make further exploration and research and translate them into other languages. Therefore, the future of translating ethnic classics is bright. At the same time, we should also realize that there are still many ethnic works which are close to extinction and urgently need to be rescued. We still have a long way to go in the fields of translation and research in ethnic classics.

(Li Zhengshuan, Standing Vice Chairman and Secretary General, Classics Translation Committee of CACSEC, PhD supervisor at Hebei Normal University)

序　二

◎王　宏

好友云南师范大学外国语学院李昌银教授来电嘱托我为“云南少数民族经典作品英译文库”的出版写一序言，并随即发来该文库的背景资料，让我“不着急，慢慢写”。我本人从事中国典籍英译及研究，深知少数民族典籍对外传译的重要性，但又是少数民族典籍翻译的门外汉。因此，我是怀着虚心学习的态度来写此序言的。近年来，在中国文化“走出去”战略工程大背景下，在中央和地方各级政府的大力支持下，我国少数民族典籍的对外传译及研究工作顺利开展，取得了很大的进步。请看以下数据：

2008 年，广西百色学院韩家权教授获批国家社科基金项目《布洛陀史诗》（壮汉英对照）。该项目已顺利结项，并于 2013 年 12 月获得中国民间文艺最高奖“山花奖”。

2012 年，广西百色学院外语系翻译团队翻译的国家级非物质文化遗产《壮族嘹歌》（英文版）由广西师范大学出版社正式出版。

2012 年，东北大学秦皇岛分校吴松林教授主编的《蒙古族系列：江格尔（汉英对照）》（上下册）由吉林大学出版社出版。

2013 年，河北师范大学李正栓教授英译《藏族格言诗》

由长春出版社出版发行。

2013年，云南财经大学崔晓霞教授撰写的《〈阿诗玛〉英译研究》收入由王宏印教授主编、民族出版社出版的“民族典籍翻译研究丛书”。

2014年，东北大学秦皇岛分校吴松林教授撰写的《满族档案文献研究》申请到国家社科后期资助，他英译的《英雄格斯尔可汗》由吉林大学出版社出版。

2014年，中南民族大学张立玉教授主持的“土家族主要典籍英译及研究”获批国家社科基金项目。

2015年，西安外国语大学梁真惠副教授撰写的《〈玛纳斯〉翻译传播研究》收入由王宏印教授主编、民族出版社出版的“民族典籍翻译研究丛书”。

与此同时，第一届和第二届全国少数民族典籍英译学术研讨会分别于2012年和2014年在广西民族大学和大连民族学院举行，参加会议的院校分布之广、与会代表数量之众、提交论文数量之多和涉及研究话题之细，十分可喜。2016年还将在中南民族大学举行第三届全国少数民族典籍英译学术研讨会。

为什么少数民族典籍的对外传译及研究工作在短短几年就受到译界的青睐，取得众多成果？我认为，这在很大程度上归于典籍翻译界乃至翻译界同仁对“中国典籍”的重新思考和认识。中国典籍浩如烟海，卷帙浩繁，举世瞩目，是全人类共同的精神财富。但对于中国典籍的理解，我们以前较多限于汉民族的重要文献和书籍，而对少数民族多有忽略。在讨论中国典籍时，也较多关注古代文学作品。其实，中国典籍指“中国清代末年1911年以前的重要文献和书籍”，这就要求我们从事典籍翻译时，不但要翻译古代文学典籍作品，还要翻译古代哲学、科技、法律、医学、经济、军事、天文、地理等诸多方面的典籍作品，不但要翻译汉民族的典籍作品，也要翻译各少数民族的典籍作品。

民族典籍具有该民族的原型符号的特质，蕴藏着能够“遗传”并不断“再生”的文化基因。民族典籍是中华传统文化的内核，同时还是中华传统文化的符号构成规则。中国是具有56个民族的多民族国家，少数民族典籍是我国少数民族勤劳与智慧的结晶，是中华文明、也是世界文明不可或缺的一部分。少数民族典籍对外传译具有跨文化交流的作用，它不但有助于更多的人了解少数民族的独特文化，而且还有助于保护少数民族文化的独特性、维持少数民族文化多样性、促进各民族团结、提升中华文化软实力等。

中国少数民族典籍涉及宗教、文学、历史、语言、医学、天文历算等领域，内容丰富，版本多样，载体特殊，传承奇特。仅以《中国少数民族古籍总目提要》为例，该书于1997年正式立项，全书总体设计约60卷、110册，目前已出版23个民族卷共20册：纳西族卷、白族卷、东乡族卷·裕固族卷·保安族卷、土族卷·撒拉族卷、锡伯族卷、哈尼族卷、回族卷·铭刻、柯尔克孜族卷、羌族卷、毛南族卷·京族卷、仫佬族卷、达斡尔族卷、土家族卷、鄂温克族卷、鄂伦春族卷、赫哲族卷、苗族卷、侗族卷、黎族卷、朝鲜族卷。该书真实地反映了我国各少数民族古籍赋存的全面情况，充实了中国的历史和文化内容，为后人探索各种文化形式的源流、揭示中国社会文化发展的轨迹提供了极为珍贵的资料，为我国乃至世界各国人文科学研究提供了一套新颖而全面的资料，对于弘扬中华民族传统文化具有深远的历史意义和现实意义。

少数民族典籍的对外传译是一项艰巨的工作，涉及将少数民族语言译成汉语、少数民族语言之间的互译和少数民族语言译成外语（主要是英语）。前两类翻译历史源远流长，最早可追溯到春秋战国时代《越人歌》的翻译，即汉、壮语之间的翻译。少数民族典籍译成外语的时间则要晚一些。据考证，维吾尔族古典长诗《福乐智慧》成书于 1069 年或 1070 年，目前尚未发现完整的原稿，只存留下来三个抄本，分别为赫拉特抄本、费尔干纳抄本与埃及抄本，其中费尔干纳抄本于 12~13 世纪用阿拉伯文纳斯赫体抄写，1914 年发现于今中亚乌孜别克斯坦纳曼干城，现存于该共和国科学院东方研究所。这是少数民族典籍译介到国外的最早纪录。少数民族典籍外译在现代有了较快发展。一些少数民族典籍，如藏族的《格萨尔王传》、蒙古族的《江格尔》和柯尔克孜族的《玛纳斯》等英雄史诗，云南彝族的《阿诗玛》、维吾尔族的《艾里甫和赛乃姆》等民间叙事长诗已先后被翻译成英语及其他外国文字，为世人所知。这对传承少数民族经典，推动中外文化交流起到了不可替代的作用。然而，还有大量的中国少数民族典籍等待我们去翻译和研究。

云南省少数民族典籍资源十分丰富。据不完全统计，云南少数民族文字文献古籍蕴藏量达10万余册（卷），口传古籍4万余种。“云南少数民族经典作品英译文库”正是依托云南省丰富的少数民族典籍资源，借助云南师范大学外国语学院强大的翻译师资队伍，在云南人民出版社的有力支持下，首次将云南少数民族经典作品成系列对外译介的大力举措。云南师范大学外国语学院对“云南少数民族经典作品英译文库”十分重视，他们首先邀请省内外少数民族语言文化研究专家对云南民族典籍和民族文化经典作品进行筛选，做到“好中选好，优中选优”，同时调配最强的翻译力量承担文库的翻译任务。我粗略看了该文库的选题，发现选题面广，覆盖范围宽，收入了云南省阿昌族、白族、傣族、纳西族、德昂族、哈尼族、景颇族、拉祜族、苗族、普米族和彝族等民族的典籍作品。云南共有25个少数民族，其中11个少数民族的典籍作品都覆盖到了，不少作品还是首次译成英文。这将彻底改变云南少数民族典籍由于对外译介数量较少，不为世界了解的尴尬局面。

对于云南师范大学外国语学院而言，把少数民族典籍英译作为翻译专业的优势特色进行建设，这将对该院的学科建设起到助推作用。“云南少数民族经典作品英译文库”所产生的翻译成果和研究成果将培养出一批优秀的典籍翻译和研究团队，凸显该院在全国的学术特色和学术影响，同时还能将翻译能力和研究能力转化为教学能力，提高云南师范大学外国语学院翻译专业研究生的培养质量，为社会输送高水平的翻译人才，有力地支撑学院翻译专业学科的建设和发展。我对云南师范大学外国语学院的翻译师资队伍较为熟悉。作为云南省唯一获得省级高校优势特色学科建设项目的外国语学院，该院具有雄厚的翻译师资力量，在云南省各高校中当属第一。多年来，该院翻译与跨文化研究团队一直承担着对外交流与合作的各种口笔译项目及任务。由外国语学院精心挑选和确定的“云南少数民族经典作品英译文库”翻译人员绝大多数都是云南省翻译领域里的知名教授或专家，有国外留学经历，且具有扎实的英汉双语语言功底，曾翻译出版多部译著和翻译作品，并且主持和参与过多项翻译项目的研究。我阅读李昌银教授发来的文库翻译人员名单，发现多名我所熟悉的知名教授、博士也在其中，感到格外放心。

“云南少数民族经典作品英译文库”的出版发行是云南省翻译界的一件大事，也是我国少数民族典籍翻译传来的又一佳音。想当年，我和“大中华文库”总协调人李林老师曾在参加全国典籍英译学术研讨会之余一起找到李昌银教授，敦促李教授向学校和同事呼吁，少数民族典籍翻译及研究是富矿，值得快挖、深挖，能早出成果，出大成果。今天，我们当年的心愿变成了美好的现实，心里感到特别高兴。再次热烈祝贺“云南少数民族经典作品英译文库”的顺利出版！

（王宏，中国典籍翻译研究会副会长、苏州大学博士生导师）

Foreword by Wang Hong

My friend Professor Li Changyin of Yunnan Normal University asked me to write a few words for the publication of *Classics of Yunnan Ethnic Groups in English Translation*. I am more than delighted to do it. As I have been doing research in English translation of Chinese classics, I know how important this work is. In recent years, substantial progress has been made in translating Chinese ethnic classics into English and introducing them to the world. Let's look at the following accomplishments.

First of all, several projects in the English translation of ethnic classics have received funding from the National Planning Office of Philosophy and Social Science. The first of these projects is *The Epic of Baeuqloxgdoh* (Zhuang-Chinese-English trilingual version), given funding in 2008 and headed by Professor Han Jiaquan of Baise University in Guangxi Zhuang Autonomous Region. In December 2013, this translation won the Shanhua Award, the most prestigious prize for folk literature and art in China. The second project is *A Study of the Manchu Archives*, written by Professor Wu Songlin of Northeastern University at Qinhuangdao and which was given funding in 2014. The third is *English*

Translation and Study of the Major Classics of the Tujia Ethnic Group, headed by Professor Zhang Liyu of the South-Central University for Nationalities, also granted in 2014.

Secondly, several English translations have been published. In 2012, *Liao Songs of Pingguo Zhuang*, has been listed as one of China's national intangible cultural heritages. It was translated by the School of Foreign Languages, Baise University, and published by Guangxi Normal University Press. Also in 2012, *Jangar* (a Chinese-English bilingual edition), edited by Professor Wu Songlin of Northeastern University at Qinhuangdao, was published by Jilin University Press. In 2013, *Tibetan Gnomic Verses Translated into English*, translated by Professor Li Zhengshuan of Hebei Normal University, was published by Changchun Press. And in 2014, *Heroic Geser Khan*, translated by Professor Wu Songlin of Northeastern University at Qinhuangdao, was published by Jilin University Press.

And thirdly, two important monographs have been published by The Ethnic Publishing House in the *Ethnic Classics Translation Research Series* edited by Professor Wang Hongyin of Nankai University. One is *A Study on the English Translation of* Ashima *by Gladys Taylor* (2013), which was the PhD dissertation of Professor Cui Xiaoxia of Yunnan University of Finance and Economics. The other is *Translation and Dissemination of the Oral Epic Manas* (2015) written by Associate Professor Liang Zhenhui of Xi'an International

Studies University.

Meanwhile, it is encouraging to see that the first conferences on English translation of ethnic classics in China have been held in Guangxi Nationalities University and Dalian Nationalities Institute respectively. Participants were both many and enthusiastic. Many papers were presented and a lot of topics discussed. The third conference will be hosted by South Central Nationalities University in 2016.

Why, then, has this field attracted so much attention from translators and scholars alike and accomplished so much in just a few years? The answer, I believe, lies in a rethinking of what constitutes Chinese classics as an indispensable part of human heritage. We used to see Chinese classics as more or less equal to the classics of the Han people, excluding works by other ethnic groups. Moreover, when we talk about Chinese classics, we focus too much on the literary works of ancient times. Yet Chinese classics actually refer to "important works and books before 1911, the year when the Qing dynasty fell, bringing an end to imperial rule". This definition requires us to pay attention not just to literary works, but also writings in other subjects, such as philosophy, science, law, medicine, economics, military affairs, astronomy, and geography, not only Han works, but writings by other ethnic groups as well.

The classical works of a nation are its archetypal symbols, the major carriers of its cultural genes. Chinese classics make up the core of Chinese tradition. The Chinese nation consists of 56 ethnic groups. Ethnic classics are an important part of not only Chinese traditional culture, but also world civilization. The translation of these works into other languages is important in that it helps to promote cross-cultural communications between China and other countries and to protect and preserve the uniqueness and diversity of ethnic cultures by making them accessible to foreign readers.

Chinese ethnic classics cover a variety of areas, such as religion, literature, history, language, medicine, astrology, and calendar, with numerous editions, special media and unique ways of transmission from generation to generation. Take, for example, *An Anthology of Chinese Ethnic Classics*, a colossal project that includes 110 volumes, 20 of which, from 23 ethnic groups, have been published. The anthology reflects the variety and quantity of China's ethnic classics and provides valuable material and resources for studying, understanding and developing Chinese culture and history in a more comprehensive and sustainable way.

The translation of Chinese ethnic classics into foreign languages is a very demanding job, involving rendering from ethnic languages to Chinese, between ethnic languages, and from ethnic languages (often via Chinese) to foreign languages. The first two types of translation can be traced back to the Spring and Autumn Period, when *The Song of the Yue People* was translated from their mother tongue into Chinese. The earliest translation of ethnic classics into a foreign language is *Wisdom of Royal Glory*, a long poem of the Uygurs, which was rendered from the source language into Arabic and is now in the Oriental Institute of Uzbekistan at Namangan. But it was not until modern times that the translation of ethnic classics into foreign languages accelerated. Noticeably, ethnic epics, such as *The Story of Prince Geser* of the Tibetans, *The Story of Jianggeer* of the Mongolians, *Manas* of the Kyrgyz, and narrative poems such as *Ashima* of the Yi people, *Alip and Salam* of the Uygurs, etc., have been published. These translations have contributed to acquainting the world with Chinese ethnic classics, but many remain to be translated.

Yunnan is rich in ethnic classics, boasting more than 100,000 volumes of written classics and over 40,000 pieces of oral literature. Relying on such bountiful resources, as a collective endeavor of the translation team of the School of Foreign Languages and Literature, Yunnan Normal University and with the help of Yunnan People's Publishing House, *Classics of Yunnan Ethnic Groups in English Translation* is the first project to translate Yunnan ethnic classics into English on a large scale. The School adheres to a professional spirit and academic standard in carrying out the project by selecting the most authoritative texts in the source language (Chinese) and recruiting the best translators from its huge faculty. The selection of the works, covering eleven of the twenty-five ethnic groups of the province, indicates expertise and insight. The implementation of the project will change the embarrassing obscurity of Yunnan ethnic classics by making them known to the world, many of them for the first time.

In light of disciplinary development, the project is of great importance, too. Participating in the translation will strengthen the academic foundation of the teachers, enrich their experience and enhance their translation skills and research ability. This in turn will help them become better teachers and thus able to educate students with higher quality. The publication of the books will add greatly to the faculty accomplishments of the School and raise the academic standing of Yunnan Normal University by taking the first step in this direction among the universities of Yunnan province.

This publication project is a great event not only for Yunnan itself, but also for China. Looking back, I remember that Professor Li Changyin, our friend Li Lin, editor of the *Library of Chinese Classics*, and I talked enthusiastically about initiating something like this in Yunnan when we attended a conference on the translation of ethnic classics in Soochow. Lin and I strongly suggested that Professor Li do it as soon as possible. Now I am very pleased to see our talk becoming reality. Again, my congratulations on the publication of *Classics of Yunnan Ethnic Groups in English Translation*!

(Wang Hong, Vice Chairman of Classics Translation Committee of CACSEC, PhD supervisor at Soochow University)

导 言

“云南少数民族经典作品英译文库”旨在将云南少数民族的经典作品翻译介绍给国外对其感兴趣的英文读者大众。随着以古代汉文经典构成的“大中华文库”的出版发行，学界正将注意力转移到民族典籍的翻译上来。民族典籍是指由民族作家创作的反应民族历史和文化的经典作品。广西、贵州、辽宁、新疆、西藏等省区的大学已经捷足先登。我们云南也理应有所作为。云南拥有全国最多的少数民族。全省25个少数民族中，有15个为云南特有民族，即阿昌族、白族、布朗族、傣族、德昂族、独龙族、哈尼族、景颇族、基诺族、拉祜族、傈僳族、纳西族、怒族、普米族、佤族。这些民族的典籍，有的是原作，有的是汉译本，构成了一个巨大的宝库，我们有义务将其介绍给国外的英语读者和学术界。问题是，先译什么？

云南所有的25个少数民族都创造了自己的经典作品，包括史诗、神话、创世故事、民谣、戏曲、山歌和丧歌，以各种形式流传于各地，总数不下10万卷，这还不包括口传文体。经过调查研究，并征求民族学专家的建议后，我们决定重点翻译史诗和神话。史诗和神话叙述的是民族起源故事，最能反映各民族哲学、历史、文化等的概貌、渊源。我们从汗牛充栋的民族史诗与神话中精选了云南阿昌族、白族、傣族、德昂族、哈尼族、景颇族、拉祜族、苗族、纳西族、普米族、彝族等 11 个少数民族的 17 部最具有代表性的经典作品。这些作品全部都是汉语译本，由既会讲母语又精通汉语的双语学者整理、翻译而成。其中有的是在节庆仪式和表演时从口语录制而来。我们没有选择用民族语言写成的文本，首先是因为很难寻找到民族语和英语俱佳的译者；其次是因为一部分典籍的民族语言文本在民间以多种方言形式流传，情节五花八门。汉语文本系专家仔细整理、翻译而成，因而更具权威性。接下来的问题是：如何译？

在我们选定的 17 部作品中，除了《白国因由》为散文体之外，其余全部为民歌韵文体，诗行长度大致相当，行末有松散押韵，无格律。译诗为诗是最起码的要求。我们遵循的原则有如下几点。

一、若原文为诗歌，译文也必须为诗歌。

二、译文尽可能完整地再现原文的思想内容和意象。

三、译文尽可能再现原文的修辞手段。

四、不改变原文每一节诗的行数，除非万不得已。

五、不使用英文的标准格律，因为原文并不是标准的格律体。采用英文的自然节奏，但诗行长短应大体一致。

六、不用韵，除非符合英文表达习惯且不损害原文内容。

我们所追求的，用苏珊·巴斯奈特的话来说就是“异地播种”，而不是直接移栽树木。关于原文的形式特征，尤其是尾韵，能再现时再现，不能再现时果断放弃。

那谁来翻译呢？本文库是云南师范大学外国语学院的集体项目，因此我们的翻译团队由本院十几位同行加上两位在职攻读翻译专业硕士学位的高校教师组成。所有译者都在高校教授翻译课程，从事翻译研究，不仅发表了翻译论文，也出版了译著。

传统上，人们通常是将外语译为母语，而不是将母语译为外语。但是这种情况正在发生改变。现在许多译者都将母语译为外语。根据耐克·帕科恩[①]和斯图亚特·坎贝尔[②]的论证，将母语译入非母语，能够达到相当高的水平。中国的情形为他们的观点提供了新的论据。中国典籍英译在19世纪由英国汉学家理雅各和翟理斯发起，20世纪在亚瑟·伟利、戴维·霍克思、波顿·沃森、约翰·闵福德、宇文所安等英美汉学家的推动下继续发展。值得注意的是，在这一过程中，旅居西方的华人学者迅速加入到了中国典籍英译的行列中。其中最著名的是辜鸿铭和林语堂。他们主动承担这个任务，因为他们认为西方汉学家的母语并非汉语，其译文往往误读汉语原文本，误解中国文化，自己义不容辞，必须为英语读者提供更忠实的英文翻译。自20世纪50年代开始，越来越多的中国大陆译者投身于典籍英译或重译。在杨宪益、许渊冲、汪榕培、王宏印、王宏、李正栓等当代翻译家和翻译理论家的积极倡导和引领下，典籍英译蔚然成风，势头强劲。许渊冲、王宏、李正栓等都在西方出版社出版了英文译著，这表明他们的英文水平达到了国际上的出版标准。

就本文库而言，我们采取了一系列保障译文质量的措施。我们要求译者尽最大努力拿出代表自己最高水平的译文。文

① 挑战公理：译入非母语. 阿姆斯特丹：约翰·本杰明斯出版公司，2005.
② 译入第二语言. 纽约：劳特里奇出版社，2013.

库的主编们对译文进行仔细研读，纠正理解偏差、语法错误以及格式上的问题。在此基础上，我们采取了一个不可或缺的步骤，请长期在我院从事英语教学工作的美国老师包琼（Joan Cecile Boulerice）对每一个译本进行逐字逐句的修改，使之更自然流畅，更符合英文表达习惯。我们尽了最大的努力。如果译文还存在什么问题，皆由我们负责，与包琼老师无关。

在这里，我们对所有给予我们宝贵帮助和支持的专家学者深表谢忱。感谢云南人民出版社的领导为文库成功申报为“十三五”国家重点出版物出版规划项目和国家出版基金项目给予的大力支持。感谢文库责编、东南亚南亚读物编辑部主任郭木玉，她的严谨和敬业令我们动容。感谢云南师范大学为文库提供了出版资金支持，使译者们不被“眼前的苟且”干扰，能够一心一意地追求“诗和远方”。感谢李正栓教授和王宏教授不仅一直鼓励我们前进，而且欣然为文库作序，从全球视野对其意义进行肯定，极大地提振了我们的信心。感谢包琼老师，她的修改保证了译文的流畅性。最后要特别感谢王宏教授和湖南人民出版社的资深编辑李林先生，是他们的建议促成了本文库的构想。

云南师范大学外国语学院

“云南少数民族经典作品英译文库”编委会

General Introduction

This publication project, *Classics of Yunnan Ethnic Groups in English Translation*, aims at introducing Yunnan ethnic classical works to the world by making them available to native speakers of English who might be interested in them. With the publication of the *Library of Chinese Classics*, which consists only of books written by Han authors in classical Chinese, attention now is being turned to the English translation and publication of ethnic classics, books produced by ethnic writers about their history and culture. Universities in provinces such as Guangxi, Guizhou, Liaoning, Xinjiang, and Xizang, have taken the initiative. We in Yunnan must do something, because Yunnan has the largest number of ethnic groups in China. 15 of the 25 ethnic groups in the province, the Achang, the Bai, the Bulang, the Dai, the De'ang, the Dulong, the Hani, the Jingpo, the Jinuo, the Lahu, the Lisu, the Naxi, the Nu, the Pumi, and the Wa, live in no other place but Yunnan. The classics of these people, either in their own language or in Chinese translations, are a great treasure house, which should be accessible to English readers and scholars. But what works should be translated first?

All the 25 ethnic groups in Yunnan have their classics,

epics, mythology, creation stories, folksongs, folk drama, mountain songs, and funeral lament lyrics, most of which exist in different versions in different places. According to one estimation, there are more than 100,000 volumes of them, excluding those in oral form. After a thorough survey and extensive consultations with experts of ethnic studies, we concluded that priority must be given to epics and mythologies, as they reflect an ethnic people's philosophy, history and culture more than anything else by narrating the stories of where and how they think they came from. From many epics and mythologies, we selected 17 of the most authoritative and popular classics representing 11 Yunnan ethnic groups, the Achang, the Bai, the Dai, the De'ang, the Hani, the Jingpo, the Lahu, the Miao, the Naxi, the Pumi, and the Yi. These works are all in Chinese, translated from the original by bilingual scholars whose mother tongue is their own ethnic language and who are fluent and proficient in Chinese. Some were recorded from their oral form at rituals and performances. We did not choose texts written in the ethnic language, not least because it is very hard to find a translator who is skilled in both the ethnic language and English. Moreover, some of the classics in the ethnic language were circulated in various oral forms and fragments. The published Chinese versions have been carefully edited and translated, hence they are more reliable. The next question is: how to translate them?

It happens that all of the 17 works except one are in verse form, with lines more or less the same length and loose rhymes, but no regular meter. A poem must be rendered into a poem; anything less is unacceptable. So here are the general rules we follow when doing the translation.

One. If the original is verse, the translated text must be verse, too.

Two. Reproduce the ideas and the images of the original as completely as possible.

Three. Reproduce the figures of speech of the original as much as possible.

Four. Do not change the number of lines in a stanza unless absolutely necessary.

Five. Do not use standard meters in English, because the Chinese original does not follow any regular meter. Use the natural rhythm of English instead, but most of the lines should look more or less the same length.

Six. Do not use rhyme unless it comes naturally and is faithful to the content of the original.

What we try to do is, to use Susan Bassnett's words, "transplant the seed", not the tree itself. As for the various aspects of form, particularly meter and end rhyme, we reproduce them when it is possible and abandon them when it is necessary.

Who will do the translations? As this is a collective project of the School of Foreign Languages and Literature of Yunnan Normal University, our team consists of a dozen faculty members and two students from our MA translation program who are already teachers in other universities. All the translators have been teaching translation and doing translation research for a long time. They have published not just academic articles on translation, but also translated books from English to Chinese or vice versa.

Traditionally, people translate into their mother tongue, not into a foreign language. But the situation is changing. Many translators today are translating from their mother tongue into a foreign language. The quality can be good, as Nike K. Pokorn and Stuart Campbell prove in *Challenging the Traditional Axioms: Translation into a non-mother tongue* (Amsterdam: John Benjamins Publishing Company, 2005) and *Translation into the Second Language* (New York: Routledge, 2013) respectively. The case of China provides further evidence for their argument. The translation of Chinese classics into English was initiated by James Legge and Herbert Allen Giles in the 19th century and carried on in the 20th century by Arthur Waley, David Hawkes, Burton Watson, John Minford, Stephen Owen and others. It is noticeable that these English and American sinologists were soon joined by Chinese scholars residing in the West, such as Hongming (Tomson) Gu and Lin Yutang, among others. They took up the job because they thought it was their obligation to give English readers more faithful translations than Western sinologists could, who, as their target language is their mother tongue, often misinterpret the original text and misrepresent Chinese culture. Since the 1950s, there has been an increasingly powerful trend for Mainland Chinese translators to render or re-render Chinese classics into foreign languages, English in particular. In our time, this work is gathering momentum, enthusiastically advocated and actively practiced by such well-known translation experts as Yang Xianyi of Beijing Foreign Language Press, Xu Yuanchong of Beijing University, Wang Rongpei of Dalian Foreign Language Institute, Wang Hongyin of Nankai University, Wang Hong of Soochow University, Li Zhengshuan of Hebei Normal University, and many more. These professors are not just translators, but also scholars in translation studies. More importantly, some of them, Xu Yuanchong, Wang Hong and Li Zhengshuan, for example, have had their translations published by Western publishers, which suggests that their English meets the international standard.

In the case of our project, we request that the translators do their best to produce good translations. When they submit them to us, they should represent the highest level that they can attain. Then the general editors appointed by the School read the translated texts and remove inaccurate renderings and grammar mistakes if there are any. On top of that, we've taken an indispensable measure to ensure that our English is readable. We asked Ms. Joan Cecile Boulerice, an American teacher who has been teaching English in our school since 2009, to read every text that we've translated and improve the English by making it more natural and idiomatic. This is the best we can do. Of course any problems that still remain in the translations are ours. They have nothing to do with our American teacher.

As the project is well under way, we would like to thank all those who have helped to make it possible. Ms. Guo Muyu, director of the South and Southeast Asia Editorial Department, Yunnan People's Publishing House, has been most helpful in our cooperation. In addition, she has added importance to the project by turning it into a national publication project. Yunnan Normal University has supported us by paying the publication fees so that the translators won't have to be burdened with the financial responsibilities for this project. Professor Li Zhengshuan and Professor Wang Hong not only have always encouraged us to go on but have also written the forewords for the project, putting it in a global perspective. Ms. Joan Cecile Boulerice's revision has ensured the fluency of the translated texts. Finally, special thanks must be given to Professor Wang Hong, again, and Mr. Li Lin of Hunan People's Press for their suggestion that has helped us conceive the project from the very beginning.

The General Editors
School of Foreign Languages & Literature
Yunnan Normal University, Kunming

娥并与桑洛

目录

* 所有标题为译者所加。

娥并与桑洛

目录

Contents

* The canto titles are added by the translator.

Contents

娥并与桑洛 Ebing and Sangluo

我要把这个古老的故事
像红烛一样来点亮，
让它的光芒射到四方……

I will light this ancient story
Like a red candle,
And let its light illuminate every place ...

一　桑洛出生

景多昂是个热闹的地方，
赶街的人来来往往，
牛马成群结队，
牛脖子上挂着铃铛。

景多昂是个快乐的地方，
到处是象脚鼓的声响，
口弦在竹楼上弹奏，
琴声在竹林里飘荡。

景多昂四面都是高山，
泉水在山间流淌，
竹楼成排成行，
楼角指着星星和月亮。

广阔的田坝，
平坦得像蝴蝶的翅膀，
一直伸到高高的金塔下，
这里住着沙铁①苏定那。

① 沙铁：因商致富的大富翁。

I. The Birth of Sangluo

Jingduo'ang was a lively place.
In the market people came and went.
Cattle and horses grazed in herds,
With bells hanging on the cattle's necks.

Jingduo'ang was a happy place.
Elephant-foot drums were heard everywhere,
Jaw harps were played in bamboo houses,
And mouth organs were blowing in bamboo forests.

Jingduo'ang was surrounded by mountains,
With springs flowing between them.
Bamboo houses were in rows and lines,
Their cornices pointing to the stars and the moon.

Wide paddy fields,
As flat as the wings of butterflies,
Extended to the feet of a tall golden pagoda.
Here lived Shatie[1] Sudingna.

---

[1] Shatie: a rich man who became rich by doing business.

沙铁的钱多得像谷子，
金子银子堆得像小山，
沙铁的家漂亮又宽广，
养着成群的牛马和大象。

沙铁没有儿女，
夫妻俩成天焦虑，
这么多的财产，
死后谁来承继？

沙铁不管天晴下雨，
天天拿上鲜花，
到奘房[①]去拜佛，
一年之后终于生了一个儿子。

沙铁夫妇高兴得不得了，
给儿子取名叫埃果那，
埃果那只活了一个月就死了，
夫妇俩哭得声音嗄哑。

过了一年又生了一个儿子，
亲戚朋友都来祝贺，

① 奘房：佛寺。

The Shatie's money was as plentiful as grains.
His gold and silver was piled like hills.
His house was big and beautiful;
He had herds of cattle, horses, and elephants.

The Shatie had no children,
Which worried his wife and him day and night.
They had such a large fortune,
But who would inherit it after their death?

No matter whether it was sunny or rainy,
The Shatie went to the Buddhist temple
With flowers to pray to Buddha every day.
One year later he finally had a son.

The Shatie and his wife were extremely happy,
And named their son Aiguona.
The son lived for only one month and died;
The couple cried till their voices became hoarse.

One year later they had another son.
All their relatives and friends came to congratulate them.

给孩子取名叫易，
易只活了两个月就死了。

夫妇俩一天到晚地悲伤，
日夜盼望再生一个孩子。
一天，沙铁的妻子做了一个梦，
梦见天上飞满星星。

一颗最明亮的星掉了下来，
落在她手上闪闪发光，
所有的亲戚朋友都跑来看望，
她忙把星星往裙子里藏。

正藏着猛然惊醒，
发现自己躺在床上。
鸡叫了，天亮了，
她把梦告诉了丈夫。

她疑惑地问：
“多么奇怪的梦啊！
快告诉我吧，
这是好事，
还是灾祸？”

The baby was named Yi.
He lived for only two months before he died.

The couple was sad from morning to night;
They hoped day and night to have one child.
One day the Shatie's wife had a dream.
In the dream the sky was full of stars.

The brightest star fell from the sky
And dropped twinkling into her hands.
All relatives and friends came to see it.
She hurriedly hid the star under her skirt.

While hiding the star she suddenly woke up,
And found herself lying in bed.
After the cocks crowed and day broke,
She told her husband the dream.

She asked him in wonder:
"What a strange dream it is!
Please tell me
Whether it foretells a good thing
Or a disaster."

沙铁说这是一个好梦，
他轻快得像被风吹起的树叶，
天天想抱上又白又胖的孩子，
他的妻子不久果然又怀了孕。

傣历三月初三，
月亮弯得像把梳子，
星星闪得特别明亮，
孩子就在这晚出世。

孩子的皮肤白得像水晶，
脸儿团团像月亮，
小嘴红得像紫椒，
父亲给他取名叫桑洛。

母亲把他抱在怀里，
喂他银白的奶；
父亲把他背在背上，
用的是绸缎的背带。

远远近近的亲戚，
姑爹姑妈舅舅，
大姐姨妈老表，
都来把桑洛称赞。

The Shatie said that it was a good dream.
He became light-hearted like a leaf flying in the wind,
Dreaming of embracing a cute baby every day.
His wife became pregnant not long after.

On March the third of the Dai calendar,
The new moon was curved like a comb,
And the stars were especially bright.
Their child was born that night.

The child's skin was as white as crystal.
His face was as round as the full moon,
His lips as red as red chilies,
And his dad named him Sangluo.

His mother held him in her arms
And fed him with milk;
His father carried him on his back
With a baby sling made of silk.

All relatives from afar and near,
All the uncles, aunts,
Cousins and nephews
Came to congratulate them.

景多昂的姑娘都来了，
小玉、小安、小娥，
争着来抱桑洛，
嘴里夸奖心里羡慕：

“小桑洛呀！
你小小的就这么漂亮，
长大了更没有人比得上；
你像迎春花一样开放，
我们已被太阳晒得枯黄。

“小桑洛呀！
你生得太迟了，
我们不能采一个园子里的花，
我们不能唱一样的歌。

“小桑洛呀！
假如你是园里的花朵，
我们要把你戴在头上；
假如你是树上的果子，
我们要把你揣在怀里。
“可惜我们相差太远，
好像大刀和斧头。

All the girls in Jingduo'ang came.
Xiao Yu, Xiao An and Xiao E,
All wanted to hold Sangluo first,
Praising and admiring him:

"Little Sangluo,
You are so young but so cute.
Nobody will be able to match you when you grow up;
You will bloom like a winter jasmine,
While we are withering in the sun.

"Little Sangluo,
You were born so late.
We cannot gather flowers in the same garden,
Nor can we sing the same songs.

"Little Sangluo,
If you were a flower in the garden,
We would wear you on our heads.
If you were a fruit,
We would hold you in our bosoms.
"It's unfortunate our ages are so far apart,
Like a broadsword and an axe.

你快快长大吧！
我们闻闻香味就够了。

“不同辈的桑洛呀！
要是你早点生下，
我们要在竹楼下纺纱，[①]
陪着你谈笑在月光下。”

就像一棵竹笋，
生长在绿茵茵的竹林里；
桑洛长得美丽，
逗得所有的姑娘欢喜。

就像荷花开在水池里，
走过的人都把它称赞；
都想在水边停留，
把它摘下带在自己身边。

二 姑娘们的爱慕

日子一天天过去，
日子一月月又来，
桑洛学会在地上爬，

① 傣族姑娘习惯在竹楼下纺纱等待情人。

Grow up quickly!
We are content just to smell your fragrance.

"Sangluo of the next generation,
If you were born earlier,
We'd spin in front of our bamboo houses,[1]
And chat with you under the moonlight."

Like a bamboo shoot
Growing in a green bamboo forest,
Sangluo was so cute
That all the girls liked him.

Just like a lotus in a pond,
Which all the people that went by praised
And wanted to stop by the water
To pick and carry away.

II. The Girls' Love for Sangluo

The days elapsed one by one;
New months were back in a new year.
Sangluo learned to crawl on the ground,

---

① The Dai girls used to spin while waiting for their lovers in front of their bamboo houses.

有时爬到谷仓里去。

七月的时候父亲死了，
母亲整天哭哭啼啼。
她把丈夫埋葬，
靠儿子来解除悲伤。

桑洛一天天长大，
长到三四岁了，
他在天井里跑来跑去，
有时候一个人跑出了大门。

很快长到十四五岁，
桑洛成了小伙子，
天一亮就离开家，
骑着马到田野里去奔跑。

太阳落山他才回家，
拴好马又背上了琴。
他弹琴就像讲话，
他讲话也像弹琴。

人人都想和他讲话，
人人都想听他弹琴，

And into the barn, sometimes.

His father died in July;
His mother cried day and night.
She buried her husband,
Relying on her son to alleviate her grief.

Sangluo grew up day by day.
When he was three or four years old,
He ran about in the courtyard,
And sometimes out of the gate.

Soon he was about fifteen,
And became a young man.
Leaving home at dawn,
He galloped his horse in the field.

He came home at sunset,
Tied up the horse and took the harp.
He played the harp as if talking,
While he talked as if playing.

Everyone wanted to talk with him;
Everyone wanted to listen to him playing the harp.

老人孩子爱听，
姑娘更爱听。

姑娘们天天盼望桑洛，
天天等着桑洛的琴声。
“只要桑洛到了我家，
我马上搬凳子给他坐下。”[①]

有的姑娘早已摆好凳子，
有的姑娘整夜在竹楼下织布，
有的靠在门边等待，
有的拿锄头去修好门前的路。

有的姑娘听说桑洛要来，
把竹门换成新的；
有的姑娘听说桑洛要来，
拿一根竹棍到楼边去吆狗。

景多昂的姑娘，
天不亮就忙着去挑水，

① 傣族习惯，姑娘们喜爱的小伙子来了，便搬最好的凳子给他坐；如果姑娘讨厌这个小伙子，便搬一个坏凳子或者根本不给他坐。

Elderly people and children liked to listen,
But girls liked to listen even more.

They were looking forward to meeting Sangluo every day,
And to hearing Sangluo's harp.
"If Sangluo comes to my home,
I'll fetch a chair for him immediately."①

Some girls had prepared chairs long ago;
Some girls had weaved in front of their bamboo houses all night.
Some girls had waited for him while leaning against the door;
Some girls took hoes to mend the road to their door.

When they heard that Sangluo was coming,
Some girls replaced the old bamboo doors with new ones;
When they heard that Sangluo was coming,
Some girls took sticks to drive away their dogs at home.

The girls in Jingduo'ang
Began to carry water before daybreak.

---

① According to the Dai people's custom, when a young man comes to a girl's home, if she likes the young man, she will fetch the best chair for him. If she dislikes him, she will fetch a broken chair for him, or not give him anything to sit on.

井边的水桶在碰撞，[1]
挑水的姑娘一行行。

为了看看桑洛，
挑水的姑娘，
故意从他家门前绕过，
桑洛的门前姑娘多，水桶也多。

桑洛长大了，
姑娘们对他更喜欢，
老年人说桑洛是自家的亲戚，
姑娘们说桑洛是妈妈的女婿。

桑洛从寨子走过，
姑娘们都把窗子打开，
心里的话呀，
不好意思说出口来。

“桑洛哥哥呀！
假如你是一朵花，
我要睡在你的花瓣下，
夜晚闻着你的芳香，

① 傣族男子从不挑水、煮饭，这些都是女子的事情。每天早晨，妇女们都到井边、河边挑水，已成习惯。

Buckets collided beside the well;[1]
Girls in rows came to carry water.

In order to have a look at Sangluo,
Water-carrying girls went by his door on purpose.
At Sangluo's door there were many girls
And many buckets.

Sangluo was grown up,
And the girls loved him more.
Elderly people said Sangluo was their relative,
While girls said Sangluo was their mothers' son-in-law.

When Sangluo walked through the village,
All the girls opened their windows.
But the words in their hearts
Were too embarrassing to be said.

"Brother Sangluo!
If you were a flower,
I'd sleep under your petals.
In the evening I'd smell your fragrance

---

① Males of the Dai ethnic group never carry water nor cook meals. These are females' duties. Every morning, women go to the wells or river banks to carry water and it is the custom of the Dai people.

早晨看着你开放。

“桑洛哥哥呀！
你要是一只燕子，
就请到我家来搭窝。
我家的屋梁最干净，
哪管你只借宿几天，
我都会喜欢得掉泪。”

小玉姑娘心里更着急，
她梳光了头发，
趁没有人在家的时候，
学当新媳妇。
一个人在屋里扭来扭去，
一不小心跌在门槛上，
碰肿了膝头。

安毕昂姑娘高高兴兴，
说妈妈就要把她嫁给桑洛，
结婚的事不用愁，
只愁出嫁那天，
应当怎样打扮。

阿佐姑娘早已戴上耳环，

And see you blooming in the morning.

"Brother Sangluo!
If you are a swallow,
Please come to my house to build your nest.
The purlins of my house are the cleanest.
I don't care if you stay only for a few days;
I'd be so excited that my tears might fall."

The girl Little Yu was even more anxious.
She combed her hair
And pretended to be a bride
When there was nobody else at home.
While wiggling in the room,
She fell on the threshold
And made her knees swollen.

The girl Anbi'ang was very happy, saying that
Her mother would soon marry her to Sangluo.
She was not worried about marrying
Except for what she'd wear
On the day of her wedding.

The girl Azuo had put on earrings long ago,

套上漂亮的手镯，
把小凳子背在背上，
学妈妈哄娃娃。

本寨的姑娘爱桑洛。
外寨的姑娘也爱桑洛，
母亲一个也不选，
偏偏选了阿扁或安佐。

三　包办婚姻

离景多昂不远，
有个景算地方，
这里也有一家沙铁，
这家是桑洛的姨妈。

桑洛的姨妈，
有两个女儿，
一个叫阿扁，
一个叫安佐。

阿扁鼻子高高的，
长得又白又细，
她常到桑洛家来玩，

And had put on her beautiful bracelets.
She had put a little stool on her back,
Imitating her mother to lull a baby to asleep.

Girls in the village loved Sangluo,
And girls in other villages loved him too.
Sangluo's mother chose none of them
Except for Abian or Anzuo.

Ⅲ. Arranged Marriage

Not far away from Jingduo'ang,
There was a place called Jingsuan.
There was a Shatie there,
And it was Sangluo's aunt.

Sangluo's aunt
Had two daughters,
One was called Abian
And the other Anzuo.

Abian had a high nose,
White skin and a slender figure.
She often came to visit Sangluo's family,

总是讨得桑洛母亲的欢喜。

阿扁好像一条蛇，
在桑洛身边扭来扭去，
就是桑洛的影子，
她也要追随。

她有换不完的新衣服，
她有戴不完的花藤圈[①]，
嘴里叫着“咪叭[②]，咪叭”，
心里想做人家的媳妇。

她脚上的藤圈，
有绳子一样粗。
她嘴里讲的，
都是别家姑娘的坏处。
她头上天天戴花，
多得发髻也插不下。
看见男人口水特别多，
走路也要扯扯裙子和衣角。

安佐也整天跟着桑洛转，

① 藤圈：傣族姑娘戴在脚上的装饰品，黑漆的，细而亮。
② 咪叭：傣语，即大妈。

Which made Sangluo's mother pleased.

Abian was like a snake,
Who often slithered around Sangluo.
Even Sangluo's shadow,
She would follow.

She had countless new clothes to change into,
And countless flowery rattan hoops[①] to wear.
While calling "Mipa[②], Mipa",
She was thinking of being her aunt's daughter-in-law.

The rattan hoops around her feet
Were as thick as ropes.
What she talked about
Was always the shortcomings of the other girls.
She wore so many flowers on her head every day
That there was no room for her hairpin.
When she saw any man, her mouth watered;
While walking she would pull at her skirt and clothes.

Anzuo also followed Sangluo all day.

---

① Rattan hoops are foot decoration for the Dai girls. They are black, paint-coated, thin and shinny.

② Mipa means "aunt" in the Dai language.

脸上的粉搽得像灰猫，
头发上扭得出油来，
天天请人写情书给桑洛。

安佐与阿扁，
就像起了锈的黄铜，
怎能与宝石相配，
怎能放进一个袋里。

这样的姑娘，
母亲偏偏欢喜，
母亲要桑洛
挑选一个做妻子。

听说桑洛母亲喜欢阿扁、安佐，
阿扁的母亲，
走起路来洋洋得意，
踩在狗尾巴上也不觉得。

每天她到桑洛家几次，
带来桑洛喜欢的东西。
母亲连忙把东西放进柜里，
桑洛看也不看一眼。

The powder on her face made her look like a gray cat.
You could get oil by wringing her hair.
She asked people to write love letters to Sangluo for her every day.

Anzuo and Abian
Were like tarnished brass.
How could they match a precious stone?
How could they be put into the same bag with a precious stone?

Such girls, however,
Were to the liking of Sangluo's mother,
Who wanted him
To choose one of them to be his wife.

Hearing that Sangluo's mother liked Abian and Anzuo,
Abian's mother
Was walking on air;
She didn't even know when she stepped on a dog's tail.

She came to Sangluo's home several times a day,
And brought everything Sangluo liked.
Sangluo's mother put these things into drawers,
But Sangluo did not want to have a look at them.

母亲要桑洛娶阿扁，
说阿扁是他家的亲戚。
整天的唠叨纠缠，
桑洛心里很厌烦：

“可爱的姑娘走在水上，
水也不会动荡；
阿扁走在地上，
竹楼都会摇晃。

“人家说，
刺都戳不痛她的脚，
她一走进花园啊，
嫩苗都要遭殃。

“她织的布，
像一朵枯萎的花，
就是她织出十朵花，
我也不会爱她。”

Sangluo's mother wanted him to marry Abian,
Saying that Abian was their relative.
Every day her nagging and pestering
Made Sangluo very disgusted.

"When lovely girls walk on water,
Water does not move;
When Abian walks on the ground,
Even bamboo houses shake.

"People say that
Even thorns cannot penetrate her feet.
When she walks into the garden,
Tender shoots will suffer.

"The cloth weaved by her
Looks like a withered flower.
Even if she could weave ten flowers on the cloth,
I wouldn't love her."

四　离开家乡

一枝花谢了，
一枝花又接着开，
桑洛的故事永远讲不完，
像月亮落下，
第二天又升起来。

景多昂很热闹，
做生意的人来来往往，
牛群叮当的铃声四处响，
桑洛的心飞向远方。

他向母亲请求，
让他出门做生意，
他愿像牛群走遍山林，
不愿像宝石关锁在柜里。

母亲听了儿子的话，
千言万语阻挡他：
“心爱的桑洛呀！
你天天和我在一起，
你像我的镜子，

Ⅳ. Leaving Home

When one flower falls,
Another flower begins to bloom.
The stories of Sangluo never come to an end,
Just like the moon sets
But rises again the next day.

Jingduo'ang was a lively place.
Businessmen came and went.
The bells of cattle were heard everywhere,
And Sangluo's heart flew to faraway places.

He asked his mother
To allow him to leave home to do business.
He would rather go over all the mountains like the cattle
Than be locked in a box like a precious stone.

Hearing Sangluo's words,
His mother stopped him with thousands of words:
"My beloved Sangluo!
You are with me every day,
Just like my mirror.

我一天也离不开你。

“家里有的是金银，
你怎么想到做生意？
家里有这么多牛马，
你怎么不骑？
家乡有那么多姑娘爱你，
你怎么不娶？

“我的儿子呀！
我爱你哟，
像爱勐欢的宝石，
你快不要这样想，
做生意是辛苦的事。”

桑洛越想越苦恼：
“我像一只小鸟被关在笼里，
只能低着头淌眼泪，
不能像鹦哥到山里去飞。

“我只想走进深山老林，
自由自在地满山跑，
可惜不能随我的心！
我像一只大象，

I can't live without you for even one day.

"There is plenty of gold and silver in the house.
Why do you think of doing business?
There are so many cattle and horses in our family.
Why don't you ride them?
So many girls in our hometown love you.
Why don't you marry one of them?

"My son!
I love you,
Like a diamond from Menghuan.
Don't think of doing business;
It's really hard to do business."

The more Sangluo thought about it, the more vexed he was:
"I am like a bird in a cage.
I could only cry with my head down;
I can't fly into the mountains like a parrot.

"I only want to go into the forest,
Free to run all over the mountains.
It's a pity I can't follow my heart!
I'm like an elephant,

被人紧紧地关在屋里。”

桑洛天天要求出去，
他用温和的语言，
向母亲苦苦请求，
母亲不得不同意。
桑洛就像脱了缰的马，
去把朋友们约齐。

景多昂的小伙子，
个个愿和桑洛在一起；
听说要到外地去，
没有一个不愿意。

大家把衣服装进箱子，
拉来黄牛装好驮子。
换上新的绳，
装好吃的米。

牛驮子一排排放好，
桑洛要出发了。
他打扮得真漂亮，
银色的长刀背在背上。

Shut up tightly in the house."

Sangluo asked to go out every day.
He spoke softly,
And asked his mother earnestly.
His mother had to agree finally.
Sangluo was like a runaway horse,
Going out to ask his friends to go together with him.

All the young men in Jingduo'ang
Wanted to go with Sangluo;
Upon hearing that they would go to other places,
No one disagreed.

They put their clothes in boxes,
And brought cows for the packages.
They replaced the old reins with new ones,
And packed rice for their own use.

When cow loads were laid in rows,
Sangluo was ready to set out.
He was handsomely dressed,
With a long silver knife on his back.

桑洛脸上闪着红光，
头上戴着三角篾帽，
太阳照着他的衣裳，
金色的纽扣也在闪光。

桑洛的马也很俊美，
脖子上的铃叮叮当当。
桑洛高高骑在马上，
金线绣的鞋子踏在镫上。

景多昂的姑娘穿得漂漂亮亮，
站在路旁送桑洛。
看见桑洛走过，
姑娘们唱起了歌：

“多好的桑洛哥哥呀！
你为什么要离开家乡？
我们的地方这样好，
你为什么想到远方？
我们从小一起长大，
难道你的爱情呵，
要到远方去寻找？

“桑洛哥哥呀！

Sangluo's face was glowing,
With a triangular bamboo hat on his head.
The sun shone upon his clothes,
And his flashing golden buttons, too.

Sangluo's horse was beautiful too,
With a bell tinkling around its neck.
Sangluo rode high on the horse;
Gold-thread-stitched shoes filled the stirrups.

The girls in Jingduo'ang were dressed beautifully,
Standing by the road to see Sangluo off.
When they saw Sangluo passing by,
The girls sang:

"Good brother Sangluo!
Why are you leaving hometown?
Our place is so good.
Why do you still want to go to distant places?
We grew up together.
Does your love
Have to be found in distant places?

"Brother Sangluo!

你像高高树梢上的一朵花，
我们这些姑娘啊，
只能抬着头白白地望着它。

“桑洛哥哥呀！
你不喜欢家乡，
你不喜欢我们，
就像森林里的小鸟，
尝到苦味的野果，
慌忙从森林里飞走了。

“墙外的金银花呀！
我们天天想把你摘下
戴在我们头上。
现在永远不能够了，
蜜蜂蝴蝶把花采走了。

“亲爱的桑洛哥哥，
你要离开我们，
就像水鸭子
不愿走进陌生的池塘。

“你像深山里的麂子，
挣断了猎人的缰绳，

You are like a flower at the top of a tall tree.

We girls

Could only look up at it in vain.

"Brother Sangluo!

You don't like your hometown,

And you don't like us.

You are like a bird in the forest

That tastes a bitter wild fruit,

And flies away in a panic.

"Every day we want to pick

The honeysuckle outside the wall,

And wear it on our heads.

Now it is impossible,

As bees and butterflies have already picked the flower.

"Dear brother Sangluo,

You're leaving us,

Like a water duck

Unwilling to enter a strange pond.

"You are like a muntjac in the mountain

That breaks away from the hunter's bridle,

飞快地跑进森林，
到更远的山里去了。

“漂亮的哥哥呀！
姑娘们的心，
像干池塘里的青蛙，
盼望着大雨快快淋下。
愿你不要忘记了家乡，
不要永远在外面流浪。

“桑洛哥哥呀！
你要离开家乡，
我们只能送点槟榔，
嚼着槟榔你就会想起我们。

“我们想念你，
我们等待你，
不要让粉红的花朵枯萎，
不要让新绣的金花褪色。
要是不怕爹妈骂，
我们一定跟着你去。

“去吧！我们无法把你拉住，
我们挡不住你的路，

And runs fast into the forest
And faraway mountains.

"Handsome brother!
Our hearts
Are like frogs in a dry pond,
Expecting it will rain soon.
We hope you won't forget your hometown,
And won't wander outside forever.

"Brother Sangluo!
You're leaving home.
We can only give you some betel nuts.
When chewing them you'll think of us.

"We'll miss you;
We'll wait for you.
Don't let the pink flowers wither;
Don't let the newly embroidered golden flowers fade.
If we were not afraid of our parents' criticism,
We'd go with you.

"Go! We can't make you stay.
We can't stand in your way.

只求你好好记住我们的话，
记住我们的祝福。

“去吧！慢慢地走吧！
不要忧愁，不要牵挂。
愿你高高兴兴地去，
愿你高高兴兴地回家。

“要是你能活一千年，
一千年也不要忘记我们；
你就是走得再远，
我们也在你身边。

“去吧！快快地去吧！
快快地回来吧！
发光的宝石啊，
不要永远让银盒子空着。”

姑娘们举手把槟榔、茶叶
递给桑洛，
露出了雪白的手臂、
银亮的手镯。

姑娘们的话，

Just remember our words;
Remember our blessings.

"Go! Go slowly!
Don't be depressed. Don't worry.
We wish you go joyfully;
We wish you come home happily.

"If you could live a thousand years;
Don't forget us for a thousand years.
No matter how far you go,
Our hearts will be with you.

"Go! Go quickly!
Come back quickly!
Shining jewels,
Don't leave the silver box empty forever."

When girls handed betel nuts and tea
To Sangluo,
They exposed their white arms
And silver bracelets.

The girls' words,

好像森林里的鸟儿叫，
叫开了岩石上的花，
桑洛高兴地回答：

“再见了，姑娘们！
我们要走了，
并不是为了离开你们，
并不是因为不爱家乡。

“亲爱的姑娘们！
愿你们在家里，
打扮得更漂亮，
歌唱得更响亮。

“姑娘们啊！你们像孔雀一样，
孔雀的美在它的羽毛上；
你们像龙银鸟一样，
龙银鸟的美在它的声音上；
你们像公鸡一样，
公鸡的美在它长长的尾巴上；
姑娘们啊！你们的美，
是在你们的心上。

“宝石一样的姑娘们啊！

Like birds' chirps in the forest,
Woke up flowers on the rocks.
Sangluo answered happily:

"Good-bye, girls!
We're leaving,
Not because I want to leave you,
Nor because I don't love our hometown.

"Dear girls!
Wish you are dressed more beautifully,
And sing better
At home.

"Girls! You're like peacocks,
And the beauty of peacocks lies in their feathers.
You're like silver dragon birds,
And the beauty of silver dragon birds lies in their voices.
You're like roosters,
And the beauty of roosters lies in their long tails.
Girls! Your beauty
Lies in your hearts.

"Jewels-like girls!

我永远记着你们，
永远不会把你们遗忘。
树林里鸟叫的时候，
我就会想起你们；
田里开始插秧的时候，
我就会回到家乡。”

桑洛骑在马上，
转回头向姑娘们招手，
铃子的声音渐渐消失，
离家的人们走远了……

五　人在旅途

天竹长大了，
笋叶一张张掉在地上。
我的歌啊！
像露水淋湿的树枝，
又发出了嫩绿的芽。

离开了景多昂，
牛铃叮叮当当地响，
牛在呜哦呜哦地叫，
吆牛的小伙子心里也高兴，

I'll remember you forever;
You will never be forgotten.
When the birds in the woods sing,
I'll think of you.
When rice transplanting begins in the field,
I'll come home."

Riding on a horse,
Sangluo looked back and waved to the girls.
The sound of bells died away;
The young men were gone away from home...

V. On the Road

When nandina domestica grow up,
Their sheaths fall one by one on the ground.
My song
Is like a dewy branch,
From which green buds grow again.

After they left Jingduo'ang,
The bells were tinkling,
And the cows were mooing.
The young cowmen were happy

在树林里唱起了山歌。

走过竹林，
又走进森林，
遇见挡路的刺丛，
用长刀把它们斩尽。

走了一整天，
太阳落山了，
桑洛和他的朋友们，
卸下牛驮子，
要在森林里住宿。

有的放牛去吃草，
有的上山去找柴，
有的泉边去淘米，
熊熊的篝火烧起来。

深山的夜，
特别美丽，
月亮忽而被树梢遮住，
忽而又从林中露出。

月亮的光照在大地上，

And began to sing folk songs.

After going through a bamboo grove,
And then into a forest,
When meeting thorns along the way,
They used long knives to clear them away.

After they walked for a day,
The sun was setting.
Sangluo and his friends
Unloaded the cows,
And planned to spend the night in the forest.

Some began to herd cows;
Some went up the hill to find firewood;
Some went to the spring to wash rice.
A bonfire was made.

The night in the mountains
Was especially beautiful.
The moon was occasionally blocked by branches,
And occasionally appeared from behind the trees.

Moonlight shone upon the ground,

照在密密的树林里，
四周静悄悄，
只有小鸟在咕咕咕地叫。

月亮又露出来了，
清凉的霜落在人们脸上。
桑洛的琴声轻轻飘起，
他歌唱可爱的家乡。

他想起门前的水井，
每天早上挤满了水桶，
挑水的姑娘们，
这时该起床了……

天蒙蒙亮，
风吹树叶哗哗响，
野鸡在山谷里啼叫，
小伙子们起身了。

没有出过门的黄牛，
走得很慢很慢，
小伙子抽了一鞭，
它又蹦蹦跳跳跑上前。

And into the thick woods.
It was quiet all around,
Except for the coos of birds.

The moon appeared again,
While cool frost formed on people's faces.
Sangluo's harp started softly,
To sing about his lovely hometown.

He thought of the well in front of the door.
Every morning there were many buckets by the well.
For water-carrying girls,
It was time to get up now...

When day broke,
The wind was blowing through the leaves.
When the wild fowl was chirping in the valley,
The young men resumed their journey.

Having never been away from home before,
The cows went very slowly.
A young man cracked a whip,
And they sped up again.

离开景多昂很远了，
又来到一个村寨。
这里的姑娘嘴是甜的，
跑来向客人问长问短：

“哥哥们从哪里来？
要到哪里去？
你们的牛真多啊，
你们牛的铃子真响啊。

“你们来到这里，
好像月亮升在天边，
可惜我们之间啊，
像太阳和月亮一样离得远。”

又走了一天，
天快黑了，
星星围着月亮，
乌云罩在山顶，
像一朵朵的花，
在森林上空飘动。

他们又走进一个寨子，
寨子边的水泉旁，

It was already a long way from Jingduo'ang,
When the young men came to a village.
The girls here were enthusiastic,
And they came out to the guests to ask questions:

"Brothers, where are you from?
Where are you going?
You have so many cows;
The bells of your cows are resounding.

"You come here,
Like the moon rising in the sky.
Unfortunately the distance between us
Is like that between the sun and the moon."

After walking for another day,
It was getting dark.
Stars appeared around the moon;
Clouds hung over the tops of mountains,
Like flowers
Floating over the forest.

They went into a village.
Beside the spring at the edge of the village,

挑水的姑娘穿梭不停，
裙子的声音沙沙悉悉，
好像在说：
“漂亮的哥哥，
去哪里？去哪里？”

她们从泉边走来，
挑着清凉的泉水，
走得那么轻盈，
好像燕子飞。

天快亮了，
牛铃在响动。
桑洛背上了腰刀，
骑上了骏马。

经过寨边泉水旁，
穿过热闹的街子，
姑娘们向桑洛问好，
水晶的耳环摇摇晃晃。

穿过一座密密的大森林，

Water-carrying girls shuttled constantly.
Their skirts were rustling,
As if saying:
"Handsome brothers,
Where are you going? Where are you going?"

They came back from the spring,
Carrying cool spring water,
Walking so lightly,
Like swallows flying.

At daybreak,
Cow bells were ringing.
Sangluo put on his broadsword,
And mounted his fine horse.

While they went by the spring of the village
And passed through busy streets,
Girls said hello to Sangluo,
Their crystal earrings dangling.

After going through a dense forest,

来到崩龙族[①]的地方。
眼前是一片绿色的茶林，
密密层层像秧田一样。

牛的铃声传到山上，
戴着银项圈的崩龙族姑娘，
背着竹篓篓，
一齐跑下山来。

按照崩龙族的风俗，
准备了丰盛的饭菜，
招待远方来的客人，
招待漂亮的桑洛。

桑洛也回送了礼物，
送的是槟榔和烟草。
崩龙姑娘又敬献了茶叶，
邀请客人们上山休息。

① 德昂族的旧称。——译者注

They came to the place of the Benglong people[1].
In front of them were green tea groves,
So dense that they were like paddy fields.

When the tinkling bells reached the hills,
The Benglong girls wearing silver necklaces
Ran down the hill together,
With bamboo baskets on their backs.

Following the custom of the Benglong people,
They prepared a good meal
To entertain guests from afar,
To entertain handsome Sangluo.

Sangluo gave them some gifts in return,
Including betel nuts and tobacco.
The Benglong girls then offered some tea
And invited the guests up to the hills to rest.

① Benglong people is the old name of the De'ang ethnic group in China. – Translator's note.

六　轰动猛根

话儿呀说不完，
歌儿呀唱不完，
像姑娘坐在织布机前，
永远织不尽那长长的线。

走了一天又一天，
第三天来到了猛根地方。
猛根遍地是鲜花，
一朵朵盛开在地上。

猛根城里很热闹，
城外流过一条大河，
河里有起伏的波浪，
河边有美丽的姑娘。

桑洛来到猛根，
像春天的泉水，
流进了城外的大河；
像好听的铓锣，
在街子上敲响。

Ⅵ. Causing a Sensation in Menggen

Stories are not finished;
Songs are not finished either,
Like a girl sitting in front of a loom,
Spinning endless threads.

After walking for two days,
They came to Menggen on the third day.
There were flowers everywhere,
All in full bloom.

Menggen was a busy city.
There was a big river outside the city.
There were rolling waves in the river,
And beautiful girls at the banks.

Sangluo came to Menggen,
Like spring water
Flowing into the big river outside the city;
Like a pleasant gong
Being played in the street.

牛群停在猛根的塔下，
猛根的人们都来接待客人。
姑娘打扮得像鲜花一样，
害羞地看着他们。

人们给商队找了舒适的住处，
男男女女都热情地来看望。
桑洛请大家尝了新鲜的茶叶，
客人的大方很快传到四方。

到了赶街天，
猛根城里的人真多，
都想来尝点茶叶，
都想来看看桑洛。

这样漂亮的青年，
猛根从没有见过，
猛根城热闹得像一条河，
人们像鱼一样来往穿梭。

猛根的姑娘都来了，
放下了装得满满的水桶，
丢下了手里织的布，
停下了转动的纺车。

The cows stopped at the foot of the pagoda of Menggen;
The people of Menggen came to meet the guests.
The girls dressed like flowers
Were looking at them shyly.

People found comfortable accommodation for them.
Men and women came to visit them enthusiastically.
Sangluo offered them fresh tea;
The generosity of the guests soon spread everywhere.

On the market day,
There were so many people in Menggen.
Everybody wanted to try some tea;
Everybody wanted to see Sangluo.

Such a handsome young man
Had never appeared in Menggen.
Menggen was as busy as a river;
People went back and forth like fish.

All the girls in Menggen were here.
They put down buckets full of water,
Left the cloth they were weaving,
And stopped their spinning wheels.

姑娘们穿着绸裙，
像水塘里的鸭子一样美丽，
嘴里嚼着槟榔，
金耳环一晃一晃。

怕羞的姑娘，
假装买东西，
慢慢从桑洛面前走过，
怕头发不好看，
一边走路一边梳头。
大胆的姑娘，
高高举着双手，
笑嘻嘻地对客人们说：
“远方的哥哥们，
我们是换东西来的。”

有的姑娘太高兴了，
把两句话也说错了：
“远方的哥哥们，
我们换你们来了。”

好吃的水果，
送给客人们尝；

Wearing silk dresses,
The girls were as beautiful as ducks in the ponds,
With betel nuts in their mouths
And dangling gold earrings.

Shy girls
Pretended to buy something,
And walked slowly in front of Sangluo.
Fearing that their hair would look untidy,
They combed it as they walked by.
Bold girls,
Holding hands high,
Said to the guests, smiling:
"Brothers from afar,
We come here to exchange some things."

Some girls were so happy
That they said wrong words:
"Brothers from afar,
We come here to exchange you."

Delicious fruits
Were given to the guests to eat;

客人们的东西，
大家争着买光。

桑洛来到猛根，
像春风吹送花香……

七　初次相会

漂亮的花苞，
一串串垂在树上。
像鲜花一样的歌啊，快开放吧！
人们等着闻你的芳香。

猛根靠着大山，
山下有河水流过，
河水流不尽，
猛根一年四季有歌声。

古老的猛根城啊，
有个美丽的姑娘，
比棉花还要洁白，
比云彩还要柔和。

手指像竹笋，

The commodities brought by the guests
Were all sold.

Sangluo came to Menggen,
Like flower fragrance brought by a spring breeze ...

Ⅶ. The First Date

Strings of beautiful buds
Hang from the trees.
Flower-like songs, bloom!
People are waiting to smell your fragrance.

Behind Menggen was a mountain,
With a river flowing at its foot.
The water of the river ran endlessly,
Just like songs in Menggen that never ended.

In the old Menggen city,
There was a beautiful girl;
Her skin was whiter than cotton,
And softer than clouds.

Her fingers were like bamboo shoots;

声音像口弦，
她会说会讲，
她的名字叫娥并。

园子里的菜，
韭菜长得最快；
猛根的姑娘，
数荷花样的娥并最漂亮。

娥并的歌声又细又轻，
全寨子的人都爱听。
小伙子们听见，
再不敢拨动琴弦。

娥并听到桑洛的消息，
她停下织机，向母亲请求：
“亲爱的妈妈，
答应我去赶街吧！
我只去一天。”

女儿要出门，
母亲不放心：
“我的姑娘啊！
你正像鲜花一样开放，

Her voice was like a jaw harp;
She was eloquent,
And her name was Ebing.

Of all the vegetables in the garden,
Leeks grow fastest.
Of all the girls in Menggen,
Lotus-like Ebing was the most beautiful.

Ebing's songs were light and gentle.
All the people in the village wanted to listen to them.
After young men heard her songs,
They did not dare to play the harp again.

After she heard the news of Sangluo,
She stopped her loom and begged her mother:
"Dear mother,
Please allow me to go to the market!
I'll go for only one day."

Seeing that her daughter wanted to go out,
The mother felt worried:
"My daughter!
You are blooming like a flower.

别到街上去吧！
我怕有人会把鲜花损伤。

“我的姑娘啊！
你像一朵娇嫩的小花，
从小开在我的花棚里，
我怕旁人会把你偷偷摘去。

“从前赶街，
叫你去你也不去；
今天赶街，
不叫你去偏要去。

“你是想买什么东西？
家里有你吃的，
家里有你穿的。

“你是要买口弦？
家里还有四五个。
每个都吹得响，
每个都吹得好听。

“你要想吃水果？
园里的果子已经成熟。

Don’t go out into the street!
I’m afraid someone may hurt the flower.

“My daughter!
You are like a delicate little flower,
Growing up in my garden.
I’m afraid someone may steal you away.

“In past market days,
You didn’t go to the market even if we asked you to.
But today,
You insist on going even if we dissuade you.

“Do you want to buy something?
We have all kinds of food for you to eat,
And all kinds of clothes for you to wear.

“Do you want to buy a jaw harp?
There are still four or five at home.
All of them are in good condition,
And every one of them can be played melodiously.

“Do you want to eat fruit?
The fruits in our garden are ripe enough.

你要想戴花？
园里的花开得正鲜艳。

“心爱的娥并啊，
听妈的话吧！
街子上没有好吃的，
街子上的果子又苦又酸。”

听了母亲的话，
娥并没有回答。
她脱下漂亮的衣裳，
把衣裳挂在栏杆上。

母亲看见女儿脱了衣服，
放心地走进屋里去了。
娥并悄悄地出了门，
走了很远又换上另一件衣裳。
她戴上鲜花和银手镯，
戴上闪光的金耳环，
口里嚼着槟榔，
她来到街上像仙女从天而降。

娥并稳稳地走在街子上，
她的衣裳闪闪发光。

Do you want to wear flowers on your head?
The flowers in our garden are in full bloom.

"My dear Ebing,
Listen to me!
There isn't anything delicious in the market;
The fruits in the market are bitter and sour."

Hearing her mother's words,
Ebing didn't refute her.
She took off her beautiful clothes,
And hung them on the handrail.

Seeing her daughter take off her beautiful clothes,
The mother went into the room in relief.
Ebing went out silently
And changed into another dress on the way.
She put on her flowers, silver bracelets,
And shining gold earrings.
While chewing betel nuts,
She came to the market like an angel.

Ebing walked gracefully in the street;
Her clothes were brilliant,

娥并走得大大方方，
头上的花啊，
引得蜜蜂蝴蝶奔忙。

街子上的人们看见她，
想买东西的人忘了买，
想卖东西的人忘了卖；
拿着秤杆的人，
忘了把秤锤挂上；
吃饭的人放下碗，
错把菜盆端起。

喝茶的人见了她，
往碗里丢进了烟草；
抽烟的人见了她，
烟叶掉了还不住地吸。

娥并东张西望，
到处寻找桑洛。
街子上一阵马蹄响，
桑洛和他的朋友赶街来了。

两块远远相隔的草坪，
今天连在一起了。

And her steps were elegant.
The flowers on her head
Attracted busy bees and butterflies.

Seeing her in the street,
The people who wanted to buy things forgot to buy;
The people who wanted to sell things forgot to sell.
The person with a scale in his hand
Forgot to hang the scale weight.
The diner put his bowl down,
But picked up a pot by mistake.

The tea-drinker who saw her
Threw tobacco into his cup.
The smoker that saw her
Kept smoking though the tobacco had fallen off.

Ebing looked around
And tried to find Sangluo.
With some hoofbeats in the street,
Sangluo and his friends came to the market.

Two separate fields
Became connected on that day.

娥并和桑洛，
今天相会了。

像河水流进海洋，
赶街的人都围在他们身旁，
都来看美丽的娥并，
都来看漂亮的桑洛。

谁也不知道他俩的心，
他们用眼睛说话；
谁也不知道他俩的心，
就像朗并会见雪加。①

娥并和桑洛，
两颗心连在一起。
爱情呵！像金色的藤，
攀在一棵树上，
扭得比丝线还紧。

桑洛回到住的地方，
悄悄拴好了马，
急忙走到河边，
驾着小船在河里划。

---

① 朗并：传说中的仙女；雪加：傣族神话中的天神之一。

Ebing and Sangluo
Met on that day.

Like a river flowing into the ocean,
They were surrounded by people in the street.
They came to see beautiful Ebing;
They came to see handsome Sangluo.

No one knew their thoughts,
As they were communicating with their eyes;
No one knew their thoughts,
Just like Langbing meeting with Xuejia.[1]

The hearts of Ebing and Sangluo
Became connected.
Love, like golden vines
Climbing a tree,
Got entwined more tightly than silk threads.

Sangluo went back to his lodge,
Tied his horse quietly,
Hurried to the riverside,
And paddled a boat in the river.

---

① Langbing: an angel in legend; Xuejia: one of the gods in Dai mythology.

娥并正站在河里洗头，
像一朵初开的荷花，
手臂像两只象牙，
小鱼在她身边游来游去。

河水哗哗地流响，
桑洛的船在水上漂荡，
桑洛的歌声娥并听不清，
娥并望着河水轻轻地唱：

“小河呵！你流轻一些吧，
让我听听桑洛的歌。”
哗哗的水声忽然消失，
桑洛的歌啊，钻进了娥并心里。

“猛根的河水呵！
你真是清凉，
甜得像甘蔗，
绿得像草地，
我想带几罐河水回家，
只怕没有福气。

“山上的瀑布啊！

Like a blooming lotus flower,
Ebing was washing her hair in the river.
Her arms looked like two ivory tusks,
With small fish swimming about her.

With water gurgling,
Sangluo's boat floated on the river.
Ebing could not hear Sangluo's voice clearly,
So she looked at the water and sang softly:

"Little river! Please flow gently;
Let me hear Sangluo's songs."
The gurgling sound of the water suddenly died away;
Sangluo's songs flew into Ebing's heart.

"Water in Menggen,
You're really cool.
You're as sweet as sugar cane,
And as green as grass.
I want to take a few cans of water home,
But I'm afraid I don't have such good luck.

"Waterfall in the mountain!

你多么明亮，
就像一面大镜子，
对着太阳在发光。

“河里的鲤鱼啊！
你躲藏在哪里？
我划过了每一个波浪，
就是为了把你找寻。

“猛根像一个天堂，
姑娘们像天上的仙女。
猛根雨后的草地，
爬满了金蚂蚁。
猛根美丽的姑娘，
比金蚂蚁还多。

“磨得发光的宝石啊！
像象牙一样洁白，
是不是你吃的不是人间的米，
才会长得这样美丽？

“娥并的名字呵！
像鲜花的花粉，
被蜜蜂蝴蝶四处传去。

How bright you are!

Like a big mirror,

You shine under the sun.

"Carp in the river!

Where are you hiding?

I have paddled past every wave,

Just to find you.

"Menggen is like heaven;

Girls here are like angels in the sky.

On the grass after the rain,

Golden ants are crawling.

Beautiful girls in Menggen

Are more than the golden ants.

"Polished precious stones

Are as white as ivory.

Is the rice you eat not grown on the earth?

Is it the reason why you are so beautiful?

"Ebing's name,

Like pollen from flowers,

Has been passed around by bees and butterflies.

哥哥像一只蜜蜂，
从远方飞来采蜜。

“哥哥从景多昂来，
就是为了串妹妹[1]，
为什么风吹荷花不摇摆？
为什么洗头的妹妹口不开？”

娥并听着桑洛的歌，
半句也没有放过。
她还怕听不清楚，
把散开的头发轻轻挽成一束。

“猛根的宝石呵！
你的光射到四面八方，
为什么心里的话，
却要搁在家里？
心里的歌应该带在身边，
随时都能唱出来。

“我的这些歌，
请你把它好好保藏。
不要沉在水底，

① 串妹妹：找姑娘玩耍之意。

I am like a bee,
Flying here from afar to gather honey.

"I am from Jingduo'ang, to court you, sister.
Why doesn't the lotus swing in the wind?
Why don't you open your mouth,
Not just wash your hair?"

Ebing listened to Sangluo's songs attentively;
Not a word was spared.
Being afraid she couldn't hear clearly,
She gently coiled her loose hair.

"The precious stone of Menggen!
Your brilliance shines in all directions.
Why are your words from the heart
Left at home?
The songs of the heart should be with you,
And you can sing them out at any time.

"My songs
Should be kept well.
Don't sink them to the water's bottom;

不要被灰尘打脏。

“我唱的这些歌，
不要让它白白抛撒。
请你把它装进心里，
请你给景多昂的哥哥一句回答。”

桑洛的歌好听，
桑洛的歌就是他的爱情。
桑洛的爱情啊！
打动了娥并的心。

好像风吹树叶，
桑洛的心不住地跳。
娥并的歌像河里的流水，
逗得桑洛的心，
像小船一样在波浪上漂。

“捉鱼的哥哥呀！
你的歌声真好听，
你身上背着弩箭，
不是要去打野兽吗？
怎么又到河里来捉鱼？

Don't smear them with dust.

"For the songs I'm singing,
Don't let them go to waste.
Please leave them in your heart;
Please give an answer to this brother from Jingduo'ang."

Sangluo's songs were melodious;
Sangluo's songs were his love.
Sangluo's love
Moved Ebing's heart.

Like a leaf in the wind,
Sangluo's heart beat fast.
Ebing's songs were like the running water of the river,
Making Sangluo's heart
Float on waves like a boat.

"Fishing brother!
Your songs are so sweet!
You have a crossbow and arrows on your back.
Aren't you going to hunt game?
Why are you fishing in the river here?

“你真像一个猎人，
手里却拿着渔网。
猎人应该到山林里去，
猎人怎么会坐在船上？

“在船上的哥哥呵！
为什么你的网只撒在水面？
是不是要叫鱼儿
自己跳进小船去？

“哥哥真会唱歌啊！
哥哥却一点不会捉鱼。
哥哥赶来了那么多黄牛，
哥哥是来做生意的。

“哥哥长得这样漂亮，
猛根没有姑娘配得上。
哥哥的歌是唱给娥并的，
这里没有一个姑娘叫娥并！”

“姑娘呀，
你像春天发芽的树叶，
又嫩又绿；
你像河边的金竹子，

"You look like a hunter,
But you have a fishing net in your hand.
Hunters should go into the mountains.
Why do you sit in the boat?

"Brother in the boat!
Why do you cast your net on the surface of the water?
Do you want the fish
To jump into the boat by themselves?

"Brother, you really sing well!
But you don't know how to catch fish.
You come here with so many cows;
You come here to do business.

"Brother, you are so handsome;
No girl in Menggen can match you.
Your songs are for Ebing,
But there isn't a girl here called Ebing!"

"Girl,
You are like a leaf in spring,
Tender and green;
You are like golden bamboo by the river,

又直又细。

“你说这里没有娥并，
你却有娥并一样的眼睛，
有娥并一样的手臂，
有娥并一样的嘴唇！

“娥并的名字，
像粉团花一样芳香。
你说这里没有娥并，
我却闻到了粉团花的香味！

“不管这里有没有人叫娥并，
不管你的名字叫不叫娥并，
天神已经把我送到你的身边，
没有得到爱情啊，
我决不回去！

“我离开了家乡，
赶着牛群到远方，
不是为了做生意，
是为了寻找心爱的姑娘。

“我到过无数的寨子，

Straight and thin.

"You said Ebing isn't here,
But you have Ebing's eyes,
Ebing's arms,
And Ebing's lips!

"Ebing's name
Is as fragrant as a hydrangea flower.
You said Ebing isn't here,
But I can smell the fragrance of a hydrangea flower!

"No matter whether Ebing is here or not;
No matter whether your name is Ebing or not;
Now that God has sent me to you;
Without love,
I will never go back!

"I left my hometown,
Driving cows far away,
Not for doing business,
But for finding the girl I love.

"I've been to countless villages;

我走过每一个山冈，
尝过山里的泉水，
尝过新鲜的茶叶，
没有一个地方，
像猛根这样美丽。

“我在家里，
时刻都想出门；
我在家里，
没有一天安静。
你好像一根绳子，
把远远的小船啊！
从景多昂拉到了猛根。”

听了桑洛的歌声，
娥并轻轻回答：
“花苞呀，一个一个挂在花树上；
鲜花呀，一朵一朵开在枝头上。
钓鱼的年轻小伙子啊，
你真会唱！
你的歌像芳香的板宝花，
香味吹在我的心上。

“我想摘下这朵花戴在胸前，

I've been to every hill;
I've drunk the spring water of the mountains;
I've tasted fresh tea;
But no place
Is as beautiful as Menggen.

"When I was at home,
I always wanted to go out.
When I was at home,
I didn't have a quiet day.
You're like a rope,
Drawing a distant boat
From Jingduo'ang to Menggen."

After hearing Sangluo's songs,
Ebing replied gently:
"Buds are on the trees;
Flowers are blooming on the branches.
Fishing young man,
You can really sing well!
Your songs are like fragrant flowers,
And their fragrance flies into my heart.

"I want to pick this flower and wear it on my chest,

怕我的衣服配不上。
我怕自己长得太丑，
我怕旁人知道，
会乱说乱讲。”

“美丽的姑娘呀！
你好像一颗发光的钻石，
我在这里找到了它，
我永远要把它托在手上。

“我的爱情，
不像货物锁在箱子里，
我要唱出来，
让姑娘知道我的心意。

“姑娘呀！难道你的心，
你的爱情，
都是锁在家里，
没有带在身上吗？

“我的爱情啊！
无法隐藏，
我不讲就要唱，
不唱就要讲。

But I'm afraid my clothes don't match it.
I'm afraid I'm not beautiful enough.
I'm afraid when others know,
They will talk nonsense.

"Beautiful girl,
You are like a shining diamond.
I've found the diamond here;
I'll hold it in my hands forever.

"My love
Is not like goods locked in boxes.
I'll sing it out,
So that you will know my heart.

"Girl! Are your heart
And your love
Locked at home
And not with you?

"My love
Cannot be hidden.
I'll either sing it out
Or say it out.

“猛根漂亮的姑娘这样多，
我爱的就是你一个。
你像高高山上的鲜花，
我穿过刺丛也要摘下。

“我离开景多昂，
离开了自己的家，
我像山巅上的鲜花，
自由自在地开放。

“我像小鸟在天空自由地飞翔，
没有谁能缚住我的翅膀。
就是母亲的笼子我也要飞出，
我的爱情要自己来找寻。”

“亲爱的哥哥呀！
如果你真喜欢这朵荷花，
你就要下水去采；
如果你真爱我，
我一定在家把你等待。”

“姑娘呀！
请把你的家告诉我，

"There are many beautiful girls in Menggen,
But you are the one I love.
You are like a flower on the high mountain.
I'll pick it even if I have to go through thorns.

"I left Jingduo'ang;
I left my home.
I'm like a flower on the mountain,
Blooming freely in my ease.

"I'm like a bird flying freely in the sky;
No one can hold my wings.
I'll fly out of my mother's cage;
I'll find my love by myself."

"Dear brother!
If you really like this lotus flower,
You have to go into the water to pick it.
If you really love me,
I'll wait for you at home."

"Dear girl!
Please tell me the address of your home.

等到太阳偏西，
我一定会来串你。

“如果不能和你在一起，
一辈子没有幸福！
如果不能同建一座塔，[①]
死也不甘心！”

“我家住在街头上，
来往的人都要经过，
做生意的人爱在门外谈笑，
小孩子们爱在门边玩耍。

“我的家在街头南边，
站在街心就能望见。
家里有几棵高高的杧果树，
快熟的果子挂在枝头。”

桑洛听见连连答应，
小船在岸边靠拢。
娥并也准备回家，
把洗好的衣服放进水桶。

① 过去傣族风习，相好的夫妻，为了下世还能再做夫妻，就积钱修一座佛塔。

When the sun sets in the west,
I'll come to court you.

"If I can't be with you,
I'll have a life without happiness!
If I can't build a pagoda with you,[1]
Even in death, I won't be reconciled to it."

"My home is at the end of the street;
People come and go by the house;
Businessmen love to chat outside the door.
Children love to play by the door.

"My home is to the south of the street's end.
You can see it from the street.
There are some tall mango trees in the courtyard,
Ripe fruit hanging from the branches."

Sangluo nodded when he heard her reply;
The boat drew close to the shore.
Ebing put the washed clothes into the bucket,
Ready to go home.

① According to the custom of the Dai people, if a couple want to be a couple again in the next life, they will save up money to build a pagoda together.

八　热恋和分别

桑洛的歌啊，
像丁香花正在开放；
日子愈长，
开得愈浓愈香。

桑洛回到住处，
只望太阳快落山，
娥并回到家，
只望月亮快升起。

她早早就坐着纺线，
纺车转得特别响，
线也纺得特别多，
装满了一个个小竹箩。

爱情啊！像天上的月亮，
怎么还不升起？
走夜路的人，
正等着你的光芒！

太阳落山了，

Ⅷ. Passionate Love and Farewell

Sangluo's songs,
Bloomed like a lilac flower;
With time passing by,
It bloomed better and its fragrance was stronger.

Sangluo went back to his lodge,
Anxiously waiting for the sun to set.
Ebing returned home,
Just hoping the moon would rise sooner.

She sat down to spin;
The spinning wheel rotated very quickly.
Much yarn was spun,
Enough to fill many bamboo baskets.

Love, like the moon in the sky,
Why haven't you risen yet?
People walking at night,
Are waiting for your light!

After the sun set behind the mountains,

桑洛背上了琴，
走到猛根街子上，
找到了娥并的家。

他轻轻弹着琴，
娥并早已听得仔细。
这不是猛根小伙子弹的，
这琴弹得多好听！

娥并停下了纺车，
拿起了口弦，
桑洛已经走到楼下，
来到她的身边。

娥并的母亲看见桑洛，
心里再不为女儿焦急。
她叫女儿快快打扫竹楼，
把远方的客人请上楼去。

娥并在火塘边铺好一床褥子：
“哥哥请褥子上坐！
只怕我家竹楼不平，
真对不起哥哥。”

Sangluo brought his harp with him,
Went to the street of Menggen,
And found Ebing's home.

He played the harp softly,
While Ebing heard it clearly.
It was not played by a local young man.
How melodiously the harp was played!

Ebing stopped the spinning wheel,
And picked up her jaw harp.
Sangluo had already entered the house,
And came to her.

When Ebing's mother saw Sangluo,
She was no longer worried about her daughter.
She told her daughter to clean the bamboo house quickly,
And to invite the guest from afar to go upstairs.

Ebing spread a cotton-padded mattress beside the fire pit.
"Brother, please sit on the mattress!
I'm afraid
The floor of our bamboo house is not smooth."

娥并拿出水罐，
给桑洛倒了一碗水：
“哥哥请喝水吧！
只怕我们家的水不甜。”

娥并捧着草烟和槟榔，
亲手递给桑洛：
“太阳落坡的时候，
我就为哥哥准备好了。”

“你家的褥子，
比我家的床还平软；
你家的凉水，
比我家的糖还甜。”

琴声停止了。
口弦弹响了：
“天神送到猛根来的哥哥呀！
凉水好喝你可以挖一条沟，
让它流到景多昂去。
猛根的花好戴呵，
你可以连根挖走，
用泉水把鲜花浇养。

Ebing took out a water jug
And poured a bowl of water for Sangluo.
"Please drink water, brother!
I'm afraid our water isn't sweet."

Ebing offered tobacco and betel nuts
To Sangluo with both hands:
"I prepared them for you,
When the sun began to set."

"Your mattress
Is smoother and softer than my bed;
Your water
Is sweeter than my family's sugar."

The harp music stopped.
The music of the jaw harp began:
"Brother sent by God to Menggen!
If the water is sweet, you can dig a ditch,
And let it flow to Jingduo'ang.
If the flower in Menggen is suitable for wearing,
You can dig out its root and take it with you,
And water the flower with the spring water.

“只怕我笨手织的粗布，
配不上哥哥的细绸缎；
只怕我采的野菜和番茄，
让哥哥吃饭时难下咽。”

“水银般的妹妹呀！
猛根的好姑娘！
桑洛各地都挑遍，
再细的绸料子，
也比不上猛根的粗布；
再苦的果子，
在猛根也会变甜。

“只怕哥哥和妹妹相隔太远，
见一次面要走三十天；
只怕妹妹是镜子里的花，
我看得见却挨不到身边。
像水里的月亮，
哥哥一伸手浪花就把月光隐藏。”

“远方的哥哥呀！
世间这样宽广，
再远的路我们也能走完。
只要心里相爱，

"I'm afraid the coarse cloth made by me
Cannot match your fine satin;
I'm afraid the potherbs and tomatoes I picked
Are not good enough for you to eat."

"Mercurial sister!
Good girl of Menggen!
Sangluo has been to many places.
Finer silk
Cannot compare with the coarse cloth made in Menggen;
Bitter fruits in other places
Become sweet in Mengen.

"I'm afraid you and I are too far apart;
It takes thirty days to walk and see each other.
I'm afraid you are a flower in the mirror
That can be seen but can't be touched.
Like the moon in water,
Its light will be hidden in waves as I reach for it."

"Brother from afar!
The world is so big;
We can finish the journey no matter how far it is.
As long as there is love in our hearts,

三百天相见一次也情愿。

“我像悬岩上的野果，
没有人来采过；
我像岩石下的花苞，
没有虫子爬过。

“我们地方的姑娘，
一句话比金子珍贵。
只要哥哥不变心，
我们的爱情呵，
没有人能够拆散！”

“猛根的花呀！
我摘下了你，
别人用鲜花我也不换。
我走过深山老林，
不让你淋着雨，
不让你在路上枯萎。
我的心啊！
要像泥土和泉水，
细细地把你栽培。”

这时，火光映着娥并的耳环，

I'm willing to meet you even if it takes three hundred days.

"I'm like a wild fruit on the cliff,
Never picked by anybody;
I'm like a bud under a rock,
Never touched by any insects.

"The promises of girls in this place
Are dearer than gold.
As long as you don't change your mind,
Our love
Cannot be broken by anyone!"

"Flower of Menggen!
Once I pick you,
I'll never exchange for other flowers.
When we walk through the mountains and woods,
I'll protect you from the rain;
I'll never let you wither on the road.
My heart,
Like soil and spring water,
Will cultivate you carefully."

At this moment, the flames in the fire pit were reflected

一闪一闪。
两人都沉默无言，
爱情已深深埋进他们心间。
爱情啊！
像粉团花一样发出芳香，
两对眼睛都为爱情发光。
爱情啊！
不怕风吹雨打，
已像扭在一起的藤子，
没有什么能拆散。

说不完的话，
表白不尽的情意，
两人的情话要是写成书，
三个粪房也装不完；
好像一个深深的井水，
舀不尽，打不干。

月亮已经西沉，
天上只剩下最后一颗星星，
火塘的火渐渐熄灭了，
天快亮了。

太阳升起来了，

On the shining earrings of Ebing.
Both of them were silent,
While love was deeply rooted in their hearts.
Love,
Like hydrangea flowers giving off fragrance,
Made their eyes glow with love.
Love,
Like tangled vines,
Resistant to wind and rain,
Cannot be broken by anything.

Endless words,
Unending expression of affection,
If written in books,
Would fill more than three temples,
And like water in a deep well,
Can never be drawn out completely.

The moon had disappeared;
Only one star was still in the sky.
The fire in the fire pit died away,
And daybreak was coming.

The sun rose,

驱散山野里的浓雾。
母亲听见了桑洛的一片真情，
她暗暗地为女儿祝福。

三天过去了，
七天八天过去了，
二十个傍晚也在爱情中消磨。
每天天快亮，
桑洛才回到住的地方。

朋友们早已知道，
大家议论纷纷，
谈着桑洛的事情。
有的跟他开玩笑；
有的好心为他祝贺；
有的说他真是幸运，
到远方找到了心爱的人；
有的为桑洛担心，
怕他的母亲知道，
会阻拦他们的爱情……

小伙子们出门太久，
货物早已卖完。
买来的东西，

And dispersed the heavy fog in the mountains and fields.
After Ebing's mother heard Sangluo's affectionate words,
She blessed her daughter in her heart.

Three days passed;
Seven days and eight days passed;
Then twenty evenings were spent in love.
Every day, Sangluo
Didn't return to his lodge until daybreak.

Friends already knew the truth;
They had a lot of words
About Sangluo's love.
Some made fun of him;
Some congratulated him;
Some said he was lucky
To have found a loved one far away;
Some were worried about Sangluo:
Lest his mother should know,
She would interfere with their love ...

The young men had been away from home too long;
Their goods had all been sold.
The goods they bought

又把牛驮子装满。

朋友们不停地劝说，
桑洛不能不听。
动身前的夜晚，
桑洛来向娥并告别：

“正开放的荷花呀！
我要回家乡去了。
我们共同栽的花，
不要让旁人摘下；
我们一起引来的泉水，
不要让旁人来汲取。

“漂亮的鲜花啊，
离开你，哥哥心里多么难过！
亲爱的姑娘，
把我俩的爱情包起来，
紧紧地锁在箱子里吧，
不要让别人抢去。

“我回家要告诉母亲，
准备好礼物骑上马再来娶你。
亲爱的娥并啊！

Were loaded up on their cows.

His friends kept persuading him to leave,
And Sangluo had to listen.
On the eve of his departure,
Sangluo came to say goodbye to Ebing:

"Blooming lotus!
I'm going back to my hometown!
The flowers we planted together,
Don't let anyone else take them away;
The spring water we tapped together
Should not be dipped into by anyone else.

"Beautiful flower!
When leaving you, how sad I am!
Dear girl,
Wrap up our love,
And lock it tightly in a box.
Don't let anyone steal it.

"I'm going home to tell my mother,
Prepare gifts and ride back to marry you.
Dear Ebing!

牢牢记住我的话吧，
我请求你送我一朵花，
让它伴着我回去。”

桑洛要回景多昂，
娥并心里多焦急：
“桑洛哥哥呀！
你要回到景多昂去。
家乡的姑娘，
又会在路边迎接你；
牛群的铃声，
会使家乡的人欢喜。

“亲爱的哥哥呀！
骑上你喜爱的马，
慢慢地回家去吧。
你什么时候离开猛根，
我的心也跟你去到景多昂。

“我俩的爱情永远不会改变，
就是天上的仙人
来和我谈情，
我也不愿意。

Remember what I said.
Please give me a flower;
Let it accompany me back."

Hearing that Sangluo was going back to Jingduo'ang,
How worried Ebing was:
"Brother Sangluo!
When you go back to Jingduo'ang,
Girls in your hometown
Will meet you at the roadside again.
The cow bells
Will make people in your hometown happy.

"Dear brother!
Ride your favorite horse,
And go home slowly.
When you leave Menggen,
My heart will go with you to Jingduo'ang.

"Our love will never change.
Even if celestial beings
Come to court me,
I will not agree.

“桑洛哥哥啊！
记住我俩的爱情吧！
到了你的家乡，
不要把我遗忘。”

天快亮了，
红公鸡伸着脖子叫，
桑洛就要离开娥并了。
他俩的心啊，
像一朵鲜花，
被摘下来丢在路上一样了。

天刚刚发亮，
猛根的姑娘都起了床。
不是去挑水，
不是去摘菜，
是听见了牛铃声，
去给桑洛送行。

有的站在园子边，
有的站在大青树下，
有的躲在篱笆后面，
有的伏在栏杆上，
看着桑洛走过去。

"Brother Sangluo!
Remember our love!
When you go back to your hometown,
Don't forget me."

The day was breaking;
The red rooster craned his neck and crowed.
Sangluo was about to leave Ebing.
Their hearts were,
Like flowers,
Picked and left on the road.

When the sky was just getting bright,
All the girls in Menggen got out of bed,
Not to carry water,
Not to pick vegetables,
But to see Sangluo off,
Because they heard cow bells.

Some were standing by the garden,
Some under big green trees,
Some behind fences,
And some against handrails
To see Sangluo walking by.

桑洛的朋友们，
取下了牛脖子上的铃铛。
桑洛的心，
闷得说不出一句话，
唱不出一句歌。

娥并站在篱笆后面，
偷偷地哭泣！
她说不出话，
眼泪一滴一滴地滚下。

桑洛走远了，
影子看不见了，
娥并忍不住哭出声来。
又怕别人知道，
用裙子捂住嘴，
泪水已把衣裙湿透。

九　遭到反对

一队牛群往回走，
没有铃声也没有人声。
牛头上绿茵茵的孔雀毛，

Sangluo's friends
Took the bells off from their cows' necks.
Sangluo's heart
Was too depressed to say a word
Or sing a song.

Ebing stood behind the hedge,
Crying secretly!
She could not speak a word,
With tears rolling down from her cheeks.

Sangluo was far off,
And Ebing could not see him anymore.
She could not help crying.
For fear of being heard by others,
She covered her mouth with her skirt,
Which became wet with her tears.

IX. Mother's Objection

A herd of cows went back home,
Without any bells or sound.
The green peacock feathers on the heads of the cows

像大雨前的森林。

路啊，弯弯扭扭，
像在鸡冠上一样难走。
森林里一片烟雾，
雀鸟也不愿飞出窝。

桑洛回到家里，
亲戚朋友都来欢迎，
有的来问外地的风光，
有的来尝点春茶和槟榔。

家里挤满了客人，
大家都有说有笑。
只有桑洛，
满脸的愁苦，
一句话也不说。

桑洛回到家呵，
琴弦再也不响，
他只想着娥并，
只想偷偷去到猛根。

“山啊！

Looked like the forest before a heavy rain.

The zigzag road,
Like a chicken crest, was hard to walk on.
The forest was full of fog;
Birds did not want to fly out of their nests.

When Sangluo came home,
Friends and relatives came to welcome him.
Some came to ask about the scenery of other places;
Some came for tasting spring tea and betel nuts.

The house was packed with guests;
People were talking and laughing.
Only Sangluo,
With sadness on his face,
Did not want to say a word.

After Sangluo came home,
His harp was no longer played.
He thought of Ebing,
And wanted to go to Menggen secretly to see her.

"Mountains!

你为什么这样高?
低下来吧，
让我看看猛根在哪里!

“云啊!
飘到猛根去吧!
去看看我的娥并，
是不是在悲伤流泪?”

桑洛整天忧伤，
什么话也不愿讲。
母亲问他是生了病，
还是做生意亏了本?
桑洛没有回答。

母亲去向他的朋友探问，
朋友们说出了真情。
桑洛的母亲知道了儿子的心事，
准备把儿子狠狠教训。

桑洛天天想念娥并，
他不理睬母亲的反复盘问。
这天趁母亲睡熟，
他又骑上马去到猛根。

Why are you so high?
Please sink;
Let me see where Menggen is!

"Clouds!
Drift to Menggen!
Go and see my Ebing.
Is she weeping with sorrow?"

Sangluo was depressed all day,
Unwilling to say anything.
His mother asked him if he was ill,
Or if he lost money in business.
But Sangluo did not answer.

His mother went to ask his friends,
Who told her the truth.
Knowing what was in his mind,
Sangluo's mother prepared to give him a lesson.

Sangluo missed Ebing every day;
He ignored his mother's repeated questioning.
One day while his mother was asleep,
He mounted his horse and went to Menggen again.

桑洛在猛根住了很久，
日子一天天过去；
娥并的脸渐渐消瘦，
她已经怀孕了。

娥并看见自己和以前不同，
她告诉桑洛：
“你不要在猛根住得太长了，
我已经怀孕了。
你快快离开猛根吧，
告诉母亲再来接我。”

“亲爱的娥并啊！
你不要发愁，
不过一个月，
我一定来接你。
我去了很快就来，
你等着我吧。”

桑洛回到家，
立刻把事情告诉了母亲。
母亲听完就变了脸，
拉开嗓子大骂：

Sangluo lived in Menggen for a long time.
As time passed day by day,
Ebing's face became thinner;
She was pregnant.

Ebing found she was different now;
She said to Sangluo:
"Don't stay in Menggen for too long,
Because I'm pregnant.
Leave Menggen quickly
To tell your mother and then come to pick me up."

"Dear Ebing!
Don't worry!
In only a month,
I'll come to pick you up.
I'll come back soon.
Please wait for me."

When Sangluo went home,
He told his mother the truth.
When she heard this she became angry,
And cursed as loudly as possible:

“不知羞耻的畜生，
我用一滴滴水、一口口饭，
白白把你喂养成人，
偏偏你要跑到外乡，
干出这种丑事情！

“我只想，
你出门会找回金银；
想不到，
你会和猛根的姑娘谈情！
亲戚家的好姑娘你不要，
偏偏去找魔鬼样的女人！

“你在我的家里，
就得听我管教，
要是再不规矩，
从此不要叫我母亲！”

母亲这样凶狠，
伤了桑洛的心。
想起善良的娥并，
桑洛再也不能容忍：

"Shameless beast!
I have been working very hard
To bring you up with water and food.
But now you have been to a distant place,
And caused such a scandal!

"I thought that
You would go out and bring back gold and silver.
To my astonishment,
You fell in love with a girl in Menggen!
You refused a good girl from our relative's family,
But pursued a devil-like woman!

"Now that you are in my house,
You have to listen to me.
If you don't behave yourself,
Never call me mother again!"

His mother's fierceness
Hurt Sangluo's heart.
Thinking of kind Ebing,
Sangluo could no longer stand it:

“老年人怎懂得年轻人的心？
年轻人怎能违背自己的爱情？
母亲的话我都听，
这件事绝不能答应！

“娥并是最好的姑娘，
娥并是最好的妻子！
你不准我娶娥并，
我偏偏要和她成亲！
如果你真不答应，
从此我不叫你母亲！”

桑洛这些话，
气白了母亲的嘴唇，
她知道儿子的脾气，
又用软言来劝引：

“妈妈的桑洛呀！
你要听母亲的话，
外地的姑娘，
不会使你快活，
外地的姑娘又丑又笨！

“她们织的一块布呀，

"How can the elderly understand the young?
How can a young man betray his love?
I will obey all of your words,
Except for this matter!

"Ebing is the best girl;
Ebing is the best wife!
You forbid me to marry her,
But I will persist in marrying her!
If you don't allow me,
From now on I won't call you mother!"

Hearing Sangluo's words,
His mother became angry and pale in the face.
She knew her son's temper,
So she tried to persuade him with gentle words:

"My son Sangluo!
Listen to me.
Girls from another place
Won't make you happy,
Because they are ugly and stupid!

"The cloth they weave

不够做一件衣服；
她们织的布，
像牛脖子一样粗。

“桑洛呀！
你出去这样久，
阿扁还是爱着你。
她聪明得像小鸟，
她织的布呀，
又结实又有花纹。

“你是景多昂沙铁的儿子，
怎么会爱上猛根的穷姑娘？
她们织的布，
作头巾也不够，
作手绢也不配。

“她们笨手笨脚，
织的丝绸呀，
看起来黑漆漆，
穿起来冷冰冰。

“远方的姑娘，
只会爱你一时，

Is not enough to make even one dress;
And it is
As coarse as a cow's neck.

"Sangluo!
You've been away for so long,
But Abian still loves you.
She's as smart as a bird.
The cloth she weaves
Is strong and patterned.

"You are the son of the Shatie in Jingduo'ang.
How can you fall in love with a poor girl in Menggen?
The cloth they make
Is neither long enough for a headscarf,
Nor good enough for handkerchiefs.

"They're all thumbs.
The silk they make
Looks pitch-black
And feels cold to wear.

"The girls from afar
Only love you for a while.

你要有了疾病，
她们就会把你抛弃。”

母亲这些话，
儿子不愿听。
桑洛一心挂念着娥并，
邻居和朋友也为他伤心。

十　娥并遇害

年轻的姑娘和小伙子们，
他俩的痛苦多么深！
好好地听吧，
我要让我的歌，
打动人们的心！

桑洛离开猛根，
娥并日夜等待，
左也不见来，
右也不见来，
腰身一天天地大了。
可怜的娥并呵！
日日盼望着，
夜夜在哭泣！

When you are sick,
They'll leave you."

Sangluo did not listen to
His mother's words.
Sangluo missed Ebing all the time;
His neighbors and friends were sad for him.

X. Persecution

Girls and young men,
How painful their love was!
Listen to me attentively!
I'll move people's hearts
With my song!

After Sangluo left Menggen,
Ebing began to wait for him to come back.
Day and night,
Night and day, he did not come.
Her waist was getting thicker day by day.
Poor Ebing!
She was waiting day after day,
And crying every night!

“桑洛哥哥呀！
你怎么到今天还不来？
当初我像荷花开放，
你每日每夜在我身旁；
是不是荷花枯萎了，
哥哥再不愿走近池塘？

“桑洛呀！
你像森林里的鹿，
不想再看见猎人！
怎么还不回到猛根？
娥并不是森林里的猎人。

“亲爱的桑洛！
我多么害羞呀，
没有什么痛苦能和我相比。
回到你的家想不起我了吧，
怎么还不来接我啊！？
如果我知道
你要离开这样久，
我一定跟着你去了！

“桑洛呀！

"Brother Sangluo!
Why haven't you come back?
When I bloomed like a lotus flower,
You were by my side every day and every night.
Is it because the lotus is withering
That you won't come near the pond?

"Sangluo!
You are like a deer in the forest
That doesn't want to see the hunter anymore!
Why not come back to Menggen?
Ebing is not a hunter in the forest.

"Dear Sangluo!
How ashamed I am!
No pain can compare to mine.
After going home, have you forgotten me?
Why don't you come and take me away?
If I had known
You would be away for so long,
I would have gone with you!"

"Sangluo!

我俩的爱情，
像结在一起的丝线那样紧。
为什么到今天，
还不见你的身影？”

痛苦啊，
像千斤重担，
压在娥并双肩！
母亲知道了也为女儿焦急：

“亲爱的女儿啊！
你已经长大成人，
你的事情由你决定，
我们不阻挡你，
快去找桑洛吧！”

娥并收拾了几件衣衫，
匆匆离开了猛根。
她第一次走这样远啊，
三个姑娘陪着她一起出门。

走过无数个寨子，
渡过无数条大江，
爬过无数座高山，

Our love
Is as tight as a knot of thread.
Why can't I see you
For so long?"

The pain,
Like a burden of a thousand *jin*
Was on Ebing's shoulders!
Her mother was also worried about her situation.

"My dear daughter!
You've grown up.
It's up to you to make decisions.
We will not stand in your way.
Go and find Sangluo!"

Ebing packed up some clothes,
And hurried away from Menggen.
As it was the first time for her to go so far,
Three girls went with her.

After passing countless villages,
Crossing numerous rivers,
And climbing many high mountains,

路啊，还是那么遥远。

路上没有桑洛的脚印，
林中不见桑洛的牛群。
粉团花一样的娥并呀！
她去问放牛的青年：

“放牛的哥哥们！
你们在这里放牛，
有没有看见桑洛？
到景多昂走哪一条路？”

“姑娘呵！
你仔细记住：
前面的路有几条，
到景多昂的路最难走。
你要走向日出的东方，
那就能找到桑洛。”

不知走了多少天，
走过了密密的森林，
走过了大石桥，
终于看见了河边高高的金塔，
娥并来到了景多昂的寨头。

Their destination was still so far away.

There weren't any of Sangluo's footprints on the road;
There weren't any signs of Sangluo's cows in the forest either.
Hydrangea-like Ebing
Asked the young cowmen:

"Cowmen brothers!
While you were herding cows here,
Did you see Sangluo?
Which way is it to Jingduo'ang?"

"Girl!
Remember this:
There are several roads ahead,
But the road to Jingduo'ang is the hardest.
Go to the east where the sun rises,
And you'll find Sangluo."

Nobody knows how many days passed
Before they went through thick forests,
Crossed big stone bridges,
And finally saw a tall golden pagoda by the river.
Ebing came to Jingduo'ang.

四个姑娘在河里洗了澡，
娥并换上新衣服，
抖了抖裙子，
戴上了鲜花和金手镯。

跟娥并来的姑娘，
头发也梳得很亮，
她们走进了寨子，
寻找桑洛住的地方。

桑洛的母亲，
早就猜到娥并要来，
心里的主意啊，
比魔鬼还要毒。

她收藏了家里的金银，
锁上了家里的箱柜，
用甜言蜜语对桑洛说：
“这几天你这样着急，
是不是娥并要来？
她来了我要请客，
家里却还没有酒菜。

“你快到河边去吧，

After the girls bathed in the river,
Ebing put on her new clothes,
Smoothed out her skirt,
And put on flowers and a gold bracelet.

The girls who came with Ebing
Also made their hair bright and tidy.
They went into the village
To look for the place where Sangluo lived.

Sangluo's mother
Guessed that Ebing was coming.
The tricks in her mind
Were more evil than those of devils.

She collected all the gold and silver of the family,
And locked them up in the family's locker.
Sweetly she said to Sangluo:
"You have been so anxious these days.
Is Ebing coming here?
When she's here, I'll entertain her well.
But there is no food or drink at home.

"Go to the river quickly

去打点鱼回来。
家里有我照顾，
她到了我替你招待。”

母亲的甜言蜜语，
儿子信以为真。
桑洛刚刚出去，
母亲就关上房门。

她找来许多竹片，
削得像针一样尖，
把竹针插在楼梯上，
插在竹墙上，
插在门上。
在装饭的盒子里，
藏起一把锋利的刀。

娥并走进了寨子，
心想着姑姑嫂嫂会来接她，
姐姐妹妹会来牵着她的手，
桑洛会来帮她背上包裹。

可是，没有一个人来接她，
也没有人和她打招呼。

To catch some fish.
I'll take care of everything at home,
And take care of her when she is here."

Hearing his mother's sweet words,
Sangluo believed her.
As soon as Sangluo went out,
His mother closed the door.

She found many bamboo chips,
Sharpened them into needles,
And inserted them into the stairs,
Into the bamboo walls,
And in the door.
In the box of steamed rice,
She hid a sharp knife.

Ebing went into the village,
Expecting that her sisters-in-law would come to meet her
And lead her to the house,
And Sangluo would come to carry baggage for her.

But no one came to meet her;
No one said hello to her.

三个姑娘陪着她，
进了桑洛的家。
家里不见桑洛的影子，
只有桑洛的母亲。
娥并恭恭敬敬对她行礼，
好言好语对她说话。

桑洛的母亲，
一句话不说，
脸酸溜溜的，
弯得像犁耙。

她一见娥并，
鼻子就翘起来。
弯弯扭扭的心啊，
像狗尾巴一样摇摆。

她去端来饭菜，
放在娥并面前。
她的脸酸得像木瓜，
她的声音装得像蜜糖：

“桑洛怎么还不回来，
是不是碰见了老虎？

The three girls accompanied her
To Sangluo's house.
There was no one at home,
Except Sangluo's mother.
Ebing greeted her respectfully,
And spoke kindly to her.

Sangluo's mother
Said nothing to Ebing.
Sangluo's mother's sour face
Was as bent as a plow.

As soon as she saw Ebing,
Her nose went up.
Her twisted mind
Had all kinds of bad ideas.

She brought some food
And put it in front of Ebing.
Her face was as sour as a papaya,
While her voice was like honey:

"Why hasn't Sangluo come back?
Has he encountered a tiger?

你不用为他着急，
先吃点饭再等他吧！

“腌菜是昨天才腌的，
你们来了正好碰上；
这些鱼啊，
都是桑洛为你预备的。”

桌上的东西，
哪里像人吃的！
帕贡菜像药一样苦，
腌鱼又生又臭。

娥并心里难过，
一口也咽不下。
看看母亲就要发怒，
她只好去添饭。
娥并不知道，
饭盒里会有尖刀；
娥并不知道，
母亲会有魔鬼的心肠。

You don't need to worry about him.
Have some food while waiting for him.

"The pickles were salted yesterday.
You have come in time;
The fish
Was prepared by Sangluo for you."

The things on the table
Didn't look like food for human beings!
The Pagong[1] was as bitter as medicinal herbs;
The salted fish was raw and smelly.

Ebing was sad in her heart
And couldn't eat anything.
Seeing that Sangluo's mother was losing her temper,
She got up to get some steamed rice.
Ebing did not know
There was a sharp knife in the rice box.
She did not know
Sangluo's mother had a devil's heart.

---

① Pagong is a kind of Dai cuisine. – Translator's note

娥并去抓饭，[1]
刀割破了她的手指，
娥并痛得昏了过去。
她急忙去开门，
门上的竹针又刺进了手心；
她靠在竹墙上，
墙上的竹针又刺进了背。

鲜红的血啊！
浸透了娥并的衣服。
三个姑娘看见，
连忙把她扶住。

娥并伤心哭，
呼唤着桑洛。
可是桑洛还在河边打鱼，
她眼前都是陌生的人。

眼泪一滴一滴落下来，
血一滴一滴掉下来。
血一直滴到楼下，
滴在楼下白公鸡身上，

① 从前傣族吃饭不用碗筷，用竹盒盛饭，用手抓着吃。

When Ebing tried to eat the steamed rice,
The knife cut her fingers.[1]
Ebing almost fainted with pain.
She hurried to open the door,
But the needles in the door pierced her palm.
She leaned against the bamboo wall,
But the needles in the wall stabbed into her back.

Red blood
Soaked Ebing's clothes.
Seeing that,
The three girls helped her to stand on her feet.

Ebing cried with sadness,
And called Sangluo.
But Sangluo was still fishing by the river,
And the people there were all strangers.

Her tears dropped down,
And her blood dripped too.
The blood dripped downstairs
Onto a white rooster,

① The Dai people used to hold food in a bamboo box and use hands and fingers rather than bowls and chopsticks when they ate.

把白公鸡都染红了；
滴在红公鸡身上，
把红公鸡都染成紫色。

桑洛的母亲指着大门，
高声骂娥并：
“我家的饭菜不好吃，
你就放下碗筷！
我家的屋子不好在，
你就快些离开！
我的儿子桑洛，
娶不上你这个媳妇。”

十一　失去孩子

娥并被赶出来了，
像牲口被主人赶出门。
猛根的姑娘啊！
她只能站在门外啼哭，
呼唤桑洛哥哥：

“我的桑洛呀！
你现在在哪儿？
你的娥并刚到你家，

And dyed it red;
The blood dripped onto a red rooster
And dyed it purple.

Sangluo's mother pointed to the door,
And shouted at Ebing:
"If the food in my house is not delicious,
Put down the dishes!
If my house is not good,
Get out quickly!
My son Sangluo
Can't marry a woman like you."

XI. Death of the Child

Ebing was driven out of the house,
Like an animal driven out by its owner.
The girl from Menggen
Could not help crying outside the door,
And calling for brother Sangluo:

"My Sangluo!
Where are you now?
Your Ebing just arrived at your home,

就被你母亲赶出来了。

“我身上流着血，
你快快来吧。
你怎么还不来啊？
为什么还不见你的影子？”

一边走，一边哭，
美丽的娥并，
哭哑了嗓子。
头发散下来了，
头巾落下来了，
耳环掉在地上，
血从手上滴到地上。

身边的三个姑娘，
一路上拾着掉下的东西；
她们跟着娥并哭，
一面哭，一面往后看：

“桑洛呀桑洛！
你的妻子从猛根来，
你的妻子遭到伤害，
你怎么不快快来看一眼！

But your mother has driven her out.

"I am bleeding;
Come quickly.
Why haven't you come yet?
Why can't I find you?"

Beautiful Ebing wandered about,
Crying all the way
Till her voice became hoarse.
Her hair was loose;
Her scarf dropped down;
Her earrings fell on the ground;
Her blood dripped from her hand to the ground.

The three girls around her
Picked up the things that fell along the way;
They followed Ebing and cried with her.
As they cried, they looked back repeatedly:

"Sangluo! Sangluo!
Your wife has come from Menggen;
Your wife is hurt.
Why don't you come to have a look!

这样生疏的地方，
我们到哪里去找你？”

三个姑娘扶着娥并，
走进一片树林，
娥并走不动了，
衣裙浸透了鲜血。

娥并呼唤着桑洛：
“刚开的攀枝花呀，
被风一吹，
花瓣纷纷散落；
刚离家的娥并呀，
遇见老虎，
快死在森林里了。

“我不愿死啊，
我不愿离开桑洛哥哥。
我的儿子还没有出世，
儿子还没有看见父亲。”

娥并昏倒过去，
孩子就在这时出世。
婴儿刚刚落地，

In such a strange place,
Where can we find you?"

The three girls held Ebing by the hand
And walked into some woods.
Ebing could not walk anymore;
Her dress was soaked with blood.

Ebing called Sangluo's name,
"The newly-bloomed Bombax ceiba
Is blown by a strong wind,
And its petals have dropped on the ground;
Ebing just left home,
And met a tiger.
Now I'm dying in the forest.

"I don't want to die;
I don't want to leave brother Sangluo.
My son is not born yet;
He hasn't met his father yet."

Ebing passed out,
And at that moment her child was born.
Just when the baby was born,

就在母亲身边死去。
三个姑娘把娥并摇醒，
在地上铺好绿叶，
把孩子放在上边。

“可怜的孩子啊！
你才出生就死去了。
没有尝到母亲一口奶，
没有得到父亲的疼爱。

“刚生下的孩子啊！
我怎舍得用泥土掩埋？
放在河里鱼要吃，
放在地上蚂蚁要搬，
放在池塘里青蛙要咬，
只好把你放在树上，
用树叶轻轻覆盖。

“亲爱的孩子呵！
你死在森林里，
灵魂不要跑到远方。
你要变成一只会唱的小鸟，
飞在一棵高高的树上，
在这里等着父亲。

It died right next to its mother.
The three girls woke Ebing up,
Put some green leaves on the ground,
And put the baby on them.

"Poor baby!
You died at birth,
Without drinking your mother's milk,
Without being loved by your father.

"Newly-born baby!
How can I bury you in the earth?
If I leave you in the river, fish may eat you;
If I leave you on the ground, ants may carry you to their nests;
If I leave you in the pond, frogs may bite you;
I have to put you on the tree,
And cover you gently with leaves.

"Dear baby!
You died in the forest,
But your soul should not run away.
You should become a singing bird,
Fly to a tall tree,
And wait for your father.

“亲爱的桑洛呵！
我们的爱情，
像一棵竹子，
被劈成两半了。
连刚长出的竹笋，
也被人铲掉。

“桑洛呀！
快骑上马，
快来到森林吧！
我见不着你，
还有一只小鸟，
会代替我啼叫……”

娥并的声音渐渐低沉，
树林里显得更寂静。
树梢上出现一只小鸟，
不停地叫：
“桑洛！桑洛！”
猛根的三个姑娘，
扶着娥并，
听见小鸟的叫声，
心里更觉凄凉……

"Dear Sangluo!
Our love,
Like a bamboo,
Has been cut into two pieces.
Even its newly-grown bamboo shoot
Has been dug out.

"Sangluo!
Mount your horse,
And come to this forest quickly!
If I can't meet you here,
There will be a little bird here
To sing for me..."

Ebing's voice grew fainter,
And the woods became more serene.
A little bird appeared at the top of the tree,
And it kept calling:
"Sangluo! Sangluo!"
The three girls from Menggen
Supported Ebing with their hands.
Hearing the little bird's singing,
They felt sadder and lonelier.

十二　桑洛殉情

桑洛还在撒网，
这天真不顺利，
没有网到一条鱼，
中午才回到家里。

走到门前楼梯下，
看见一缕缕的血迹，
桑洛问母亲：
“地上怎么会有血？
是哪家孩子割破了手指？”

“儿呀！
今天我煮红皮树，
想给你的娥并染布，
染水倒在地上，
到处都染红了。

“你妈妈煮了紫胶，
装在罐子里，
被娃娃们打泼在楼梯上，
看起来好像人的血迹。”

Ⅻ. Death for Love

Sangluo was still fishing,
But nothing went well that day.
He didn't catch a fish
Before he went home at noon.

When he came to the stairs in front of his house,
He saw some drops of blood.
Sangluo asked his mother:
"Why is there blood on the ground?
Whose child cut his finger?"

"My son!
Today I boiled some red tree barks,
To dye cloth for your Ebing.
The water spilled on the ground,
And made the ground red everywhere."

"I made some purple glue
And put it in a jar.
Some children spilled the glue on the stairs.
It looks like human blood."

母亲的话是在骗他，
桑洛心里一片惊疑，
他赶忙去问邻居，
邻近的人讲了实话：
“桑洛呀！
今天真是好日子，
喜事来到你家。
大象自己走到你家，
你家没有把它拴起来，
它又回到森林去了。

“一只羽毛闪亮的金孔雀，
已经飞上了你家的凉台。
可惜啊！
被你妈用箭射伤了，
金孔雀流着血飞走了……”

桑洛的心像着了火，
他跳上马就往寨外奔跑，
鞭子不停地把马抽打，
心里像有一盆火正在烧烤。

只见路上的血迹，

Sangluo was shocked that
His mother was lying to him.
He hurried to ask his neighbors,
Who told him the truth:
"Sangluo,
Today is a great day.
A happy event happened in your house.
The elephant came to your house by itself,
But your family didn't tie it up,
So it went back to the forest."

"A golden peacock, with shining feathers,
Flew to your verandah.
It was a pity that
Your mother wounded it with an arrow,
And it flew away bleeding ..."

Sangluo's heart was on fire;
He jumped onto his horse and ran out of the village.
He kept whipping the horse,
As if there were a fire burning in his heart.

What he saw on the road was blood,

不见娥并的影子，
沙地上有一群小孩，
桑洛向他们打听：

“孩子们呀！
在热辣辣的太阳下，
这里有没有人走过？
是男是女快告诉我。”

“骑马的哥哥呀！
我们什么也没有看见，
只有三个姑娘，
扶着一个姑娘走过。

“四个姑娘都漂亮，
她们来时头上戴着鲜花，
她们去时哭声响遍树林。
最漂亮的姑娘周身流血，
像只受伤的金孔雀。”

“她们过去多久了？
能不能追得上？”
“只要你的马跑得快，
不久就能赶上。”

Rather than Ebing.
A group of children were playing in the sand.
Sangluo asked them:

"Children!
In the hot sun,
Did anyone pass by here?
Please tell me quickly."

"Brother on horseback!
We didn't see anyone,
Except three girls, who
Holding another girl by the hand, went by.

"The four girls are beautiful.
They came with flowers on their heads,
And went back with their cries echoing in the woods.
The most beautiful girl was bleeding all over,
Like a wounded golden peacock."

"How long have they been gone?
Can I catch up with them?"
"As long as your horse runs fast,
It won't be long for you to catch up with them."

她们走过的河，
河水还是浑的，
河水还没有变清，
岸上还有她们的脚印。

桑洛催打着马，
又跑了一段路。
前面有个老大爹，
肩上扛着锄头。

“老伯呀，
你种田的时候，
看见有什么人走过？
请快告诉我。”

“不见，不见！
只有一朵鲜荷花，
去景多昂时开得正茂，
回来却被太阳晒焦，
花和叶子都变黄了。”

桑洛听了这些话，
心里更加难过。

At the place where they crossed the river,
The water was still muddy;
The water was not clear yet.
Their footprints were on the shore.

Sangluo whipped the horse,
And ran for some time.
There was an old man on the way,
With a hoe on his shoulder.

"Uncle,
When you worked in the field,
Did you see anybody passing by?
Please tell me quickly."

"No, no!
I only saw one fresh lotus flower.
It was in full bloom when it went to Jingduo'ang,
But it came back withered by the sun;
The flower and leaves had turned yellow."

When Sangluo heard these words,
He felt even sadder.

他抽打着马，
使完了所有的力气，
来到树林里。
一只小鸟在树上不停地叫：
“桑洛父亲，
桑洛父亲，
你来迟了！
你来迟了！”

小鸟是桑洛的血肉，
小鸟的叫声使桑洛伤心。
他在树下呆呆望着，
眼泪像夏天的雨水。

这是娥并生孩子的地方，
地上的树叶还是绿油油的；
小鸟在树上啼叫，
只是不见娥并。

“亲爱的姑娘！
等我一下吧，
再大的痛苦，
你也不要死去。

He whipped the horse
With all his strength.
When he came into the woods,
A little bird was crying on the tree:
"Father Sangluo,
Father Sangluo,
You're late!
You're late!"

The bird was composed of Sangluo's flesh and blood;
Cries of the bird grieved Sangluo even more.
Looking at the bird from under the tree,
His tears fell down like summer rain.

This was the place where Ebing gave birth to the baby;
The leaves on the ground were still bright green.
The little bird was singing in the trees,
But he could not find Ebing.

"Dear girl!
Please wait for me a while.
No matter how much pain you are in,
You must not die.

“你要等着你的桑洛，
我在马上像火烧，
痛苦无论多大，
你也要活着。”

桑洛抽打着马，
眼泪不停地流，
来到猛根，
泪水已浸湿了鞍头。

跑进寨子什么也看不见，
只见娥并家门口挤满了人。
姑娘们正在舂米，
姑娘们正在劈柴。

桑洛下马就问：
“姑娘们为什么舂米？
姑娘们为什么劈柴？”

“我们舂米不是为了别的，
是为了桑洛的娥并；
我们劈柴不是拿去卖，
是为了你的娥并。
她前脚踏进门，

"You have to wait for your Sangluo.
On horseback as if I am on fire.
No matter how much pain you are in,
You have to stay alive."

While Sangluo whipped the horse,
His tears kept running down his face.
When he got to Menggen,
His tears had soaked the saddle.

Running into the village he saw nothing
But crowds of people in front of Ebing's house.
Some girls were pounding rice;
Some girls were chopping wood.

When Sangluo dismounted his horse and asked:
"Why are you pounding rice?
Why are you chopping wood?"

"We are pounding rice not for other reason,
But for the sake of Sangluo's Ebing.
We don't chop wood to sell;
We chop wood for your Ebing.
When she stepped in the door,

后脚还没进，
就倒下地死去了。”

桑洛听见这些话，
天地都黑暗了。
他冲进娥并的屋子，
冲开挡路的人，
就像钻进了蜂房，
人们的哭声比打雷还响。

娥并的母亲坐在屋角流泪，
娥并静静地睡着，
还像活时一样美丽。
桑洛一下扑上去，
他抱起娥并，
痛苦地呼唤：

“醒醒吧！醒醒吧！
快伸开你的双手，
抱住你的桑洛；
快接住我的手帕，
擦去脸上的泪珠。

“我的好娥并！

With her second foot still out of the door,
She fell down and died."

When Sangluo heard these words,
Everything around him looked dark.
Thrusting aside the people in the way,
He rushed into Ebing's house,
Which, Like entering a hive,
Was full of people's cries.

Ebing's mother sat in a corner weeping.
Ebing lay motionless, as if she was still sleeping,
Looking as beautiful as when she was alive.
Sangluo threw himself at Ebing,
Picked her up,
And called bitterly:

"Wake up! Wake up!
Open your arms
To hold your Sangluo;
Use my handkerchief
To wipe tears from your face.

"My dear Ebing!

你为什么紧紧闭着眼睛，
桑洛在和你说话，
你为什么不回答？

“你像天上栽的荷花，
芳香的荷花怎能凋谢？
你的哥哥啊！
没有修一个竹篷，
挡住夏天的雷雨。

“黑黑的头发，
黑黑的眉毛，
像棉花一样柔和的娥并呀！
即使你不能原谅我，
也要等一等我。

“像山一样的爱情，
被狂风吹倒；
留下桑洛一个人，
活着也不再有生命！

“如果你不能等待，
那就让我们的爱情，
像大青树的根子，

Why do you keep your eyes closed?
Sangluo is talking to you;
Why don't you answer me?"

"You are like a lotus in the sky.
How can the fragrant lotus fade away?
Your brother Sangluo
Did not build a bamboo canopy
To keep out summer thunderstorms.

"Black hair,
Black eyebrows,
And as soft as cotton. Ebing!
Even if you won't forgive me,
Please wait for me.

"Mountain-like love
Is blown down by the wind;
Leaving Sangluo behind alone,
It is now meaningless to live!

"If you can't wait,
Then let our love,
Like the roots of the great green tree,

在深深的泥土里生存。”

娥并的眼睛，
微微张了三下，
看到了自己心爱的桑洛，
微笑着死在桑洛手上。

桑洛痛苦地呼唤，
双手紧紧把娥并拥抱：
“心爱的娥并啊，
你等等我吧！”
桑洛抽出了长刀！

大家慌忙拉他的手，
他抓出衣袋里的银子，
撒了满屋满地。①
人们拥着去拣，
桑洛举起了刀……
倒在娥并身边。

① 傣族习惯，人死后要撒钱，拣得钱象征平安。

Live in the deep earth."

Ebing's eyes
Opened slightly three times.
After seeing her beloved Sangluo,
She died in his arms with a smile.

Sangluo cried miserably,
Embracing Ebing tightly with both hands.
"My beloved Ebing!
Please wait for me!"
Sangluo pulled out his long knife!

All the people hurried to grasp his hands.
He took out the silver from his pocket,
And threw it all over the floor.[①]
When people hurriedly pushed to collect the money,
Sangluo raised his knife ...
And fell beside Ebing.

① According to the Dai people's customs, people used to scatter money at the death of someone. Picking up money at the occasion symbolized safety.

十三　化星续情

在一个长满青草的山坡，
有两个青年的坟墓，
人们叫作娥并山，
那里埋葬着娥并和桑洛。

为了让两个情人永难相见，
桑洛的母亲把坟墓也隔断，
放了三筒竹子隔开棺材，
用挑水的扁担挡在中间。

但是，爱情却隔不断，
好像娥并生前打水的井，
至今还没有枯干，
井水变得更甜。

水井旁有棵大青树，
树上还挂着娥并的腰带，
挑水的姑娘们，
常在树下怀念。

两个坟头上

XIII. Transforming into Stars

On a grassy slope,
There are two lovers' graves.
The hill is called Hill Ebing.
Ebing and Sangluo were buried there.

To keep the two lovers from ever seeing each other,
And to separate the tombs from each other,
Sangluo's mother planted three bamboos between the graves,
And placed a carrying pole between the coffins.

But the love between them could not be separated.
The well where Ebing drew water
Has never dried up.
The water from the well is even sweeter.

There is a big green tree by the well,
And Ebing's girdle is hung on the tree.
The girls who come to carry water
Often miss her while under the tree.

Thick reeds used to grow

长起密密的芦苇。
芦苇的根连在一起，
芦苇的花絮在一起飞。

桑洛的母亲见了，
放一把火烧了芦苇，
火光中升起两颗星星，
这就是桑洛与娥并。

一颗星出现在黄昏，
一颗星出现在黎明。
年年三月[1]两颗星相会在一起，
它们是那样明亮、美丽。

① 此处指傣历三月，为汉族农历腊月。

On the two graves.
The roots of the reeds tangled together;
Their catkins flew together too.

When Sangluo's mother saw that,
She started a fire to burn the reeds.
Two stars rose from the flame,
And the stars were Sangluo and Ebing.

One star appears at dusk,
While the other appears at dawn.
Every March[1] the two stars will meet.
They are so bright and beautiful!

---

① March here refers to the third month in the Dai calendar. It is the twelfth month in the Chinese lunar calendar.

译后记

《娥并与桑洛》是一部广泛流传在云南德宏、西双版纳、耿马等傣族聚居区的优美生动的叙事诗。同时它也是一个反抗包办婚姻而失败的凄美爱情悲剧。《娥并与桑洛》在傣族人民中有着极其深远的影响，在德宏傣族中更是家喻户晓。可以说，《娥并与桑洛》就是傣族人民的《梁山伯与祝英台》。

此次英译采用的《娥并与桑洛》汉语版本系由云南省民族民间文学德宏调查队收集整理、云南人民出版社于1978年出版。该诗由十三个部分组成：一　桑洛出生；二　姑娘们的爱慕；三　包办婚姻；四　离开家乡；五　人在旅途；六　轰动猛根；七　初次相会；八　热恋和分别；九　遭到反对；十　娥并遇害；十一　失去孩子；十二　桑洛殉情；十三　化星续情。全诗以完整的情节和鲜明的语言特色详细地描写了桑洛追求自由与反抗包办婚姻的故事，在许多方面还保留着傣族口头传说的优美细节和传统，是研究傣族民间文学与傣族文化不可或缺的重要作品。

在动笔翻译之前，在老同学叶自林先生的帮助之下，译者前往玉溪市拜访了《娥并与桑洛》1978年版主要整理者之一的杨千成先生，就原文中的个别标点符号问题和内容向他请教，获益良多，在此谨向杨先生表示真诚的感谢！

刘德周

Translator's Afterword

Ebing and Sangluo is a beautiful and vivid narrative poem widely circulated in the Dai communities in Dehong, Xishuangbanna and Gengma, Yunnan Province, China. Meanwhile, it is a sad and beautiful love tragedy about the failure to resist an arranged marriage. It has had a profound influence on Dai people and it is even a household name among the Dai people in Dehong. It is a Dai people's *Liang Shanbo and Zhu Yingtai.*

The source text of *Ebing and Sangluo* was edited by the Dehong Collecting Team of Yunnan Ethnic Folklore and published by Yunnan People's Publishing House in December, 1978. The narrative poem includes thirteen cantos: I. The Birth of Sangluo; II. The Girls' Love for Sangluo; III. Arranged Marriage; IV. Leaving Home; V. On the Road; VI Causing a Sensation in Menggen; VII. The First Date; VIII. Passionate Love and Farewell; IX. Mother's Objection; X. Persecution; XI. Death of the Child; XII. Death for Love; XIII. Transforming into Stars. With a complete plot and distinctive linguistic features, the poem describes in detail the story of Sangluo's pursuit of freedom and resistance to an arranged marriage. The beautiful attention to details and traditions of the Dai oral legends is presented throughout the poem, which makes the poem an indispensable work for studies in the folk literature and culture of the Dai people.

Before starting the translation, with the help from Mr. Ye Zilin, one of my former college classmates, I went to Yuxi city to visit Mr. Yang Qiancheng, the chief collator of the poem. I consulted him concerning several questions on the content of the poem and one punctuation mark mistake in the source text. Hence I would like to offer my sincere thanks for his help.

Liu Dezhou

译者简介

刘德周，云南师范大学外国语学院教授。近期作品包括两部专著（《反射区理论研究实践》和《英汉同语修辞格的对比研究》）和数篇学术论文。参与了多本著作和教材的编写和编辑工作。教学和科研工作之余，参与了国内外200多场国际会议的同声传译工作，在业界享有盛誉。

About the Translator

Liu Dezhou is a professor of English in the School of Foreign Languages and Literature at Yunnan Normal University. His recent publications include two monographs, *Studies and Practice of Reflexology* and *A Contrastive Study of Tautology in English and Chinese* and several articles in academic journals. He also participated in the translation or editing of several books and textbooks. Professor Liu is an experienced simultaneous interpreter and he has interpreted in over 200 international forums, workshops and seminars for many international organizations and Chinese ministries, departments and organizations in his spare time.

优佳学案

道德与法

九年级全一册（人

案

道德与法治

九年级全一册（人教版）

云南省教育出版研究所 组编

云南出版集团公司

云南教育出版社

7-5599-1225-1

介：23.70元

教材研究所研究员，原任人民教育出版社数学室主任。

冯　刚　著名数学特级教师，全国优秀教师，原任北京市海淀区教研室主任，长期从事小学数学教学研究、名教师培养和特长生培训工作。

周启欣　中国人民大学附属中学著名英语特级教师。

梁　侠　北京师范大学附属实验中学特级教师，北京市政治学科带头人，教育部思想政治课课程标准研制组成员，高中思想政治新教材编者。

刘淑梅　人民教育出版社编审，课程教材研究所研究员，原任人民教育出版社地理室主任。

李文鼎　人民教育出版社编审，课程教材研究所研究员，人教版新课标化学教材编写者，原任人民教育出版社化学室副主任。

高建军　长沙市第一中学著名生物特级教师，硕士生导师，全国模范教师。